The Dream Dredger

Also by Roberta Silman

Blood Relations (stories)
Boundaries (novel)
Somebody Else's Child (for children)

Roberta
Silman

*The
Dream
Dredger*

a novel

Persea Books • New York

For information, address the publisher:

Persea Books, Inc.
225 Lafayette Street
New York, New York 10012

Library of Congress Cataloging-in-Publication Data

Silman, Roberta.
  The dream dredger.
  I. Title.
PS3569.I45D7 1986   813'.54   86-16933
ISBN 0-89255-111-9

I wish to thank the John Simon Guggenheim Memorial Foundation and the National Endowment for the Arts for their generous support while I was writing this novel. And special thanks to Patricia Berens, Janet Gardner, and Karen Braziller for their steadfast belief in this book.

Honeywell is a fictional town, and the characters in this novel are fictional, as well. Any resemblance to persons living or dead is purely coincidental.

I am indebted to the following books on the Hudson River, which proved invaluable: *The Hudson River,* Edgar Mayhew Bacon (New York: G.P. Putnam, 1903); *The Hudson River,* Robert Boyle (New York: Macmillan, 1971); *The Hudson,* Carl Carmer (New York: Farrar & Rinehart, 1939); *The Tavern Lamps Are Burning,* Carl Carmer (New York: David McKay, 1964); *Life Along the Hudson,* Allan Keller (New York: Sleepy Hollow Restorations, 1976).

Grateful acknowledgment is made to Random House for permission to use lines from Stephen Mitchell's translation of "The Panther" by Rainer Maria Rilke.

The publication of this book was supported in part by a grant from the National Endowment for the Arts.

For Bob

You taught me to believe in dreams. And, thus, I was the dredger.

—Anne Sexton

The Hudson is . . . a river of lost dreams.

—Carl Carmer

Contents

The Dream Dredger

Diny, 1980

My mother's name was Lise Hurwitz Branson. The day after she disappeared, my brother Gil and I went to stay with our aunt and uncle in the next town. Eight hours later we learned that she was dead. Of an accident, the police said. No more. I called our father, Murray Branson, in Japan where he was giving a series of lectures, and then we waited for him to come home. During that interminable day, the psychiatrist who had taken care of my mother for almost fifteen years telephoned and asked if he could come and see us. Our Uncle George said yes. George is my father's youngest brother, and at that time he was not more than a few years older than I am now. Shocked and confused by my mother's mysterious death, George must have welcomed the doctor's offer of help. For surely this man, Henry Farnsworth, would know what to say to an eighteen-year-old girl and a fifteen-year-old boy whose mother had vanished from this earth.

Farnsworth looked exactly as he had when I saw him twice before—once, when I was about eight, and again, two years earlier, when I was sixteen. Dressed in heathery tweeds with elbow patches, white buck shoes, his thick shock of white hair a startling contrast to his slightly flushed skin and crackling blue eyes. A man you could have confidence in.

He greeted us elaborately, calling us Gilbert and Diane, though we have been known as Gil and Diny since we were small. Then he began by praising my mother: saying what a wonderful woman she was, what a superb mother, how intelligent, how competent, how beautifully she always behaved, even how lovely looking she was. But soon he began to say other things, peculiar things: how she was an immigrant, a refugee, how she had suffered so much, how she was not able to help herself, how she was in pain.

I sat straighter and concentrated on his words, which came slower and slower. Drawn-out, deliberate words that tunneled their way through George and Joanna's home as if it were a cave: "took pills every day, sometimes a few times a day," "needed to see me," "never got over her father's death," "was hospitalized years ago," "very sick after your brother Arthur died," "never seemed to be able to accept it," "didn't know if we were going to be able to help her," "managed to function and lead a normal life," "had some very rigid notions," "but then the pain became too much for her," "all she could do was stop the pain."

What was this man talking about? You stop the pain by going to the doctor, which my mother did, or into the hospital where they helped you. When I had my appendix out the pain was so bad that I screamed and my parents took me to the hospital. I could still feel my mother's arms around me and our breaths steaming together in the cold car and the soft nap of the blanket and her palm smoothing my matted hair away from my forehead, and then the doctor's face with sparkles dancing off his glasses and his deep voice saying, "Here, this will do it, this will make you feel better." Then waking up in a room with a blue-white light above me and everyone mumbling because they were wearing masks and my father smiling and my mother still smoothing my hair because that's what you did when you wanted to make sure someone didn't die.

That was how you got rid of the pain.

"But if the pain is so great, so enormous that there is no help for it but to take the most extreme measures . . ." Farnsworth's voice droned on, then hung in the air, going nowhere, and I wished I could stand up and grab those syllables that had just left his lips and were as diaphanous as bubbles of saliva; maybe if I could feel them in my hands then I would understand what they meant.

". . . and for some people the only way to get rid of the pain is to take their own life." His voice slowed down, then stopped. When he opened his mouth again, I fixed my eyes on it. "For some people the only way out is to kill themselves. To commit suicide."

Farnsworth's words lay like stones on the floor. If I opened my eyes I was sure I would see them permanently carved into the carpet or on the slate hearth or wherever they had landed. But before I could do that, I heard a low gurgling sound, and when I blinked, I saw the flash of Gil's body lunging for the doctor.

"You're a goddamned son-of-a-bitch liar! You don't know what you're talking about, making up all that garbage about her being a refugee and not being able to take care of us. She spoke better English than you do, and she was a wonderful mother, just like everyone else's, better than everyone else's, there wasn't a single thing wrong with her, you didn't even know her, how could you know her when you only saw her a few times a month and half the time she didn't even feel like going to see you? She used to tell us she went because she felt obligated, didn't want to hurt your feelings. You didn't know that, did you? You bastard. You couldn't, because you didn't even know her!

"You're just a bastard liar, that's what you are, making everyone think that all she cared about was her father or Arthur, when they're dead, and the only thing that mattered to her was Diny and me and Daddy. She always said that, and she tells the truth, not like you!"

I couldn't believe he was shouting like this—Gil hardly ever shouted at all—but this was his voice, and now Dr. Farnsworth's eyes were widening and widening as if they would burst. And then Gil was out of his chair and going for the doctor again, but this time George's hands were clamped on Gil's wrists and Farnsworth was shuffling backward out of the room and I was trembling as I felt my brother's skinny shoulders under my arm. When Gil lifted his eyes, their brown seemed to sear the air. But beneath that searing pain was something else. Gil wasn't looking or listening for Mommy anymore.

When my father walked off the plane several hours later, I expected him to be old or shriveled or perhaps suddenly as white haired as Dr. Farnsworth. But the man who waved to us was still the handsomest man on the plane or in the airport, and as he walked toward us his tall body had its usual grace. Yet when he came closer and I saw his eyes, I knew that, like us, he would never be the same. The person he had loved most in the world was gone, and my father's intense black eyes were stunned as he gathered Gil and me into his long, lanky arms.

Unlike Farnsworth, my father never believed my mother's death was a suicide although he let the police report stand: "Accident. Possible suicide. History of mental illness." I am not sure exactly what he thought even to this day, but as he talked to Gil and me during the spring and summer and fall that followed, I realized that a lot of what Farnsworth had so awkwardly told us was, incredibly, true. As I watched my father's face, I understood that he had been expecting an "accident" every day of his life since my mother's first psychotic episode.

I couldn't understand it. I heard the words and saw my father's pain, yet I could not understand that the woman I loved so much, the woman whose laughter would echo in my ears for years and years, the mother I adored and who had lived what seemed to me to be a normal, even cheerful life, was also—what? Crazy?

Not ranting and raving crazy, but crazy enough to take her own life. Or at least that's what most people seemed to believe.

For, unbeknownst to Gil and me, she had had a history of mental illness since our older brother, Arthur, had died. And part of her illness was the absolute and irrational fear that Gil and I might discover the truth about her. If we did, she was convinced, we would never be able to love her and grow up normally. So my father had agreed to a life of half-truths, evasions, even downright lies. All in the name of love—actually a great love, a rare love between two people for each other and their children.

For years I simply did not speak of my mother's death. After our experience with Farnsworth, Gil and I refused to go to see a psychiatrist, and I told myself: Your mother died, *how* is no one else's business, she's dead, that's all that anyone has to know, and it's not such a big deal. You're not the only person in the world whose mother died when you were young, you will survive.

And I did. And so did Gil. We went to college, we married, Gil had a child, we visited our father, and each year the three of us went to visit my mother's grave.

We would go in November, around the time of her birthday, when the burnished light lingers longingly, as if it knows it will soon die, and the almost leafless trees glow with a pinkish-golden tinge that has nothing to do with the sunshine spilling on our backs and necks. After we had repeated the kaddish and the other ritual prayers, we would turn and stare out at the Hudson River, which was so much a part of my mother's life, and then we would let our eyes absorb that greenish, elastic sheen that always settled on its surface late in autumn. One or another of us would usually remark that we were standing near where the *Henry Clay* burned in that tragic, senseless fire more than a hundred years ago, and soon we would cock our heads toward the short bark of a gull or the whoop of a jay, or, if it had been a mild fall and it was late enough in the day, to the repeated wistful cry of a whippoorwill.

Every November, as we walked to the car with the straight steel track of the railroad on our right and the wide band of shimmering water on our left, I could see my mother's face hanging in my mind, and I could feel her with us. For, over the years nothing has faded, as it is supposed to. No, if anything, her memory has become stronger.

Her luminous gray eyes stare at me through my dreams, her high, lilting voice and so many of the other voices in her life tumble into my head. She gave us so much joy, and yet she must have suffered so much. How was it possible for her to lead such a divided life? And why didn't we ever suspect?

What is the real story? I have begun to ask myself, now that I am married and pregnant with my first child. As I grow heavier and heavier with this baby, I am haunted by my mother's spirit, by my memories of her. For the details of my mother's life and death—which are really one and the same—provoke such love and wonder, yet so much anger and sadness as well. Why? And if I could gather all that I know and tell it, will I ever be able to approach the truth?

Europe, 1931

1

A molten, mercurial radiance fills the air, as the warm September sunlight pours from a dazzling sky, spangling the curves of horns, trumpets, tubas; lighting small fires everywhere. Lise cranes her neck to catch as many as she can, then looks beyond the instruments and the musicians to the shimmering, blue-black ripples of the Aachen See. Her upper lip is beaded with perspiration, her armpits are clammy, and her jacket—wool, middy style—imprisons her in its close weave. But she doesn't want to have to do all the twisting and turning necessary to get out of it herself, and her mother seems to be miles and miles away, in the midst of that clutch of women her father has dubbed "the matrons," who are here every year when they return to Pertisau and who stare at Lise and her brother Leo and never stop asking them questions.

Suddenly Lise hears her father whisper to her, and miraculously he frowns and lifts that heavy jacket from her shoulders and folds it inside out and places it neatly under his arm. Then he ties her hair back with a ribbon she has found in her pocket. No wonder she was suffocating, in that blue serge, with all that reddish-brown hair cascading down her back. Now, in just a loose white overblouse and her hair off her neck she feels free, a tiny girl of ten and a half who, because of her small, fine bones, could be taken for eight.

Finally, "The March Militaire," the band's farewell. When the musicians lift their hats, their brows are rimmed with shining red lines. It's far too hot for uniforms, too, especially ones like these, so heavily swagged in braid.

"Hurry, children, time to catch the steamer," her father calls. They are taking a boat ride to Jenbach where they will catch a train back to Pertisau, for one last treat of this year's holiday. Lise's sleeves puff as she moves, then she feels her mother's gloved hand in one of hers and her father's thick palm in the other. With a gentle swing, they lift her up the ramp onto the steamer, and once more she feels people's eyes on her, and she hears her mother murmur, in French, "I hope it doesn't turn her head, all these people staring at her," but Lise says nothing; her parents don't know she and Leo can understand French, their private language.

She closes her eyes as the gleaming white steamer floats into the water with the gracefulness of a swan. By now the edges of the air are turning chilly and she is glad of her jacket. As they land, Leo pulls the ribbon from her hair and as it billows behind her she hears, "Look at the color of that child's hair!" Then, "Never mind her hair, did you see her face?" and once again Lise sees her mother turn to her father, but this time Mama's eyes are pleading, begging, as if what she wants were somehow connected to all this praise for her child. But Papa doesn't seem to see; his lips are set in an unfamiliar, severe, straight line.

What is happening? Lise wonders.

Back at the hotel the two children sit in their parents' room and watch the tilted white triangles of the sailboats glide to their moorings. Behind that waltz of the sails are bruised, black-and-blue clouds. Across from them Papa reads the paper; as usual he is frowning. In the corner Mama leans into the dusty skirt of the dressing table and examines her face in the cloudy mirror, then applies some cream—the first step in the intricate process that will render her features so mysterious, almost dirty to Lise.

Soon Lise and Leo pick up the cards, and in a few moments Lise knows she will be able to lean forward and maybe stick out her tongue at her older brother and say, "Gin!" as her aunts and uncles have taught her to. But before that can happen she hears her father clearing his throat. He has put down his paper and is staring straight ahead, his eyes more forbidding than she has ever seen them, the tips of his long fingers thoughtfully brushing his beard. Something sad is coming; she can smell it. Then her mother turns, the kohl brush in her hand. Leo rises and stands next to the window.

Each figure is as still as a statue, and the only movement in the room is the flickering ocher light in the mirror where it reflects the setting, bloody sun.

"I have something to tell you, *Kinderle,*" Papa says in a whisper more tender than Lise has ever heard. Then he clears his throat again. And in that moment Lise thinks: that moment of stillness, of fear, surely she imagined it. Don't her aunts always say there isn't another child in all of Austria with an imagination like hers? Surely they are going to hear something ordinary—a new housekeeper, perhaps, or a new nurse for Papa's office, or even a new car.

But no.

"We are going back to Vienna only for a little while," her father begins. "We have sold the house and all our furniture and will have time only to pack our clothes and our special, favorite things. In two weeks' time we will be on our way to America."

All Lise knows about America is that one aunt and uncle learned how to play gin rummy there.

Suddenly all sorts of things come clear: why her parents didn't care that she and Leo were missing school, why the results of last year's Reichstag election were discussed so endlessly, why her mother has looked at these Karwendel mountains that surround Pertisau as if she were etching them onto her brain forever, and why there have been all those apprehensive glances today.

Now Lise understands. She sits back in her chair and closes her eyes; perhaps it will be easier to bear if her eyes are closed. But then all she sees is her room, her stuffed animals guarding her pillow, her desk glittering through the lacy pattern of sunshine and curtain, the *Girl With the Watering Can* over her dresser, and the huge armoire that had belonged to her mother when she was a girl. For a second Lise is convinced she will die. How can she leave that room?

But then she sees Mama's pleading eyes: Please be reasonable, don't make a fuss, everything will be all right, you'll see. Lise nods silently, and slowly the four of them begin to move again, a family preparing to go out to dinner. Before long her mother is wearing the smoky face she wears in restaurants and for company, and Leo looks a little smug as he always does when someone has told him a secret, and her father still looks a little worried way back in his eyes, but only someone who loves him can see it. A stranger would see only that he is tall and straight and smiling, proud of his family. By the time they are shown to their table at the restaurant, parents and children look almost normal; nothing seems to be out of place.

Slowly Lise seems to be floating into a fairy tale. The restaurant is decorated to look like a carousel, with pink cloths and red candles and candy-striped walls; as if in a trance Lise sips her radlermas,* then stuffs herself on chicken kiev and linzertorte. When she has to get up she's so full and sleepy she can hardly walk.

But outside, the unexpected cold slaps her in the face. Winter isn't far away in these Austrian mountains. And what about America? She stares at the patch of moonlight that is flooding the deserted square. Her life has changed utterly since this morning's concert, and now she hears the echoes of the music thumping in her ears. Beyond the square the Aachen See gleams: a huge polished stone in the darkness.

"Oh, Papa," she sighs and takes her father's blunt-fingered hand, "it's such a beautiful lake."

"I know, Liselotte, but there will be lakes and rivers, too, in America. Better than we have here. Bigger, much bigger."

Then Arthur Hurwitz vows, silently, to find them a home near water. Under the circumstances, it seems the least he can do.

2

After the holiday in Pertisau, Lise understood the true meaning of what had happened last spring. She had been home with an earache and a sore throat for several days

---

*Radlermas is a native drink: half lemonade, half beer.

and then, finally, the pain had lessened and the fever had abated. After lunch her mother came in and dripped the warm soothing Auralgan, that mysterious, pain-relieving liquid in its dark brown bottle, into Lise's ears, and then Mama said she was going out to do her marketing. Bertha, the housekeeper who had come when Leo was born, was downstairs resting, and Lise was to rest, too.

"I should be back in about an hour, darling," Mama said as she gathered the books Lise had read to return them to the library. Lise had almost finished *The Secret Garden,* and she knew that Mama would bring her some more books this afternoon. There was that, at least, to look forward to. She was trying to smile bravely at her mother despite the ache that had begun to throb, again, in her ears. Then she lay back into the pillows and watched her mother unconsciously tidy up the room as she moved, her hands never still as she straightened the sheets and blankets, then the things on Lise's night table.

"What would you like for supper?" Mama asked. Then Lise answered with all her favorite foods. But it was a game, and they both knew Lise's dinner would be soup and a boiled egg and tapioca for dessert.

"But this sore throat can't last forever," her mother reassured her, and then she was at the door to the airy room, which had just been painted—almost white with a tinge of peach. Lise had picked the color herself. Mama's eyes surveyed the walls and ceiling briefly before they rested on Lise's face. Quickly her mother hurried back for one more kiss, a swift kiss on the forehead which didn't fool Lise for a moment. It was more than a kiss, it was Mama reassuring herself that the fever, which had been danger-ously high for the last two days, was finally down.

Lise let the pain try to seep from her brain and scalp

and through her hair. High on the pillows she could feel herself slipping into a strange lightness as the puffy white clouds outside the window began to whirl slightly and the costumer in the corner of the room, which was usually hung with her school clothes for the following day, began to lift its empty self into the air and float as quietly as a summer breeze across the pastel room. Exhausted, Lise fell asleep.

When she awoke later—was it minutes or an hour?— her father was standing over her, looking worried. Had the fever shot up again? Was she desperately sick once more? Lise wondered.

"I hate to wake you, Liselotte, but I need your help," Papa was saying to her as his eyes swept the room in a nervous, unsettling way—not at all like his usual steady glance. "Can you put on your robe and slippers and come with me to my office?"

Frightened, Lise put her feet on the floor, remember- ing to put on socks before he could remind her, and was pulling the belt of her robe around her waist as she followed her father down the hall. They went down the back stair- case, the old servants' staircase of the spacious three-story house in Grinzing, a suburb of Vienna. Silently, they hur- ried along the corridor that connected the house to her father's office.

In Papa's examining room, which had a couch and examining table and the old green-tiled stove that had been in the original kitchen of the house and her father's medical books and the pictures that she and Leo had drawn for him from the time they were little, in this examining room that could pass for another living room if you took out the examining table, sat her father's old friend and teacher, Ernest Wahrhaftig. But instead of being dressed in his usual dark suit and vest with the keys to all his honorary societies hanging along his ample front, Professor Wahrhaftig was wearing a white gown that covered him to his knees. Below that were two spindly, bloody legs with welts across the calves and some flesh coming from somewhere (Lise couldn't tell and didn't want to stare too hard) and hanging loose from just above his thin, lonely-looking ankles.

Her first impulse was to look away. It didn't seem right, her seeing the old professor so undressed, almost naked. And those terrible wounds, how had they gotten there?

"Professor Wahrhaftig had some chest pains and he became faint and he fell," Papa told her in a whisper, then handed her some bandages to hold while he wrapped up the wound on Wahrhaftig's head, a surface wound and nothing like what was happening on his legs. Then Papa said quietly, "Do you think you're brave enough to help me with the cleaning and bandaging of the legs?"

Lise sucked in her lip and nodded, then realized that the pain in her ears was suddenly gone.

Some of the flesh Papa cut off, some of it he sewed back on, as Professor Wahrhaftig sat there and looked at Lise, sometimes trying to smile, sometimes wincing from the pain that had to be excruciating when the iodine hit those open sores or when the needle wove in and out of the raw flesh. If he could be so brave, then surely she couldn't cry, Lise thought.

Toward the end of the procedure, Professor Wahrhaftig's eyes began to have a glimmer of their usual life as he murmured, "Such old legs. Such old legs to suffer such absurd indignities."

Only after they were done and Wahrhaftig had been

helped, painfully, into his clothes and was walking stiffly with a cane that her father had provided, did Papa turn to her and say, "Thank you, Liselotte, but you mustn't say a word about this to anyone. After all, we don't want to scare Mama or Mrs. Wahrhaftig."

She stared. Her father was lying. He had to be. Both her mother and the professor's wife knew about the chest pains. Lise had heard the four of them discuss Professor Wahrhaftig's heart condition many times. Besides, no one could hurt himself that way from falling. The head, maybe, but not those flayed, bloody legs. No, those legs had been beaten, Lise now realized. She had had enough Dickens read to her to know beaten legs when she saw them.

But when she lifted her eyes to her father's face and saw his sad, worried eyes, she knew that she was being pledged to secrecy. And although Papa never asked her to, for the rest of that week, each afternoon when Mama went out and Bertha was resting, Lise would appear in her father's office to help with the painful process of changing the bandages. She even feigned more of an earache until the wounds began to heal and Professor Wahrhaftig began to make a few small jokes and Papa could handle the whole business by himself.

And then, because she knew she had to, Lise put it from her mind. Until that night in Pertisau when Papa told them his plan. Then she knew that the brown shirts whom Papa hated and talked about so much must have beaten up Professor Wahrhaftig. Or maybe it was Hitler, himself. Lise could not bring herself to ask, but at least she could put the two things together. And her suspicions were confirmed about a year later, on the first night of Passover in their new country, when her father confessed to his wife and children and the relatives who had come for the Seder that, indeed, Wahrhaftig had been beaten up by some brown shirts. "They were young thugs who didn't like it when Ernest said, 'Foolish boys, to be wearing that ridiculous uniform. Don't you know that he's a crackpot?' "

Her father shook his head, then continued, "They fell on him like a pack of dogs. I ran and found a policeman around the corner, and surely he saved Ernest's life. But when I saw that policeman's face, the resignation in his eyes, I knew we were in for it and that we had to leave. So did Ernest."

But even while he was telling the story of how Ernest had come to his office every day to get the wounds cleaned, Papa never gave Lise away. What she had done for him and his old friend would remain a secret until she chose to tell it, years and years later, to her own children, long after Papa and Wahrhaftig had died.

3

When Simone Hellman met Arthur Hurwitz at the beginning of 1913, she was seventeen years old. It never occurred to her that this tall, bearded, already well-known physician was in his early forties; he looked no more than thirty, possibly thirty-five. But when Simone came home and announced that she was going to marry Arthur Hurwitz, the most eligible bachelor in the professional Jewish community in Vienna, her older sisters, Gertrude and Clara, who were already married, refused to take her seriously. Still, they knew how stubborn she could be, so they took a cruel, but necessary tack.

"What would Arthur Hurwitz want with a baby like you?"

"Why would someone as intellectual as he want to

waste his time with a schoolgirl? You know, he's a friend of Ernest Wahrhaftig and it has been said that he knew Klimt and was at the railroad station with him when a bunch of them went to say goodbye to Mahler. What on earth do you think you would have to say to someone as brilliant as Arthur Hurwitz? 'Do you prefer taffeta to satin?' " And then they would laugh. Even their mother, a quiet and timid old lady (for Simone was a child of her middle age), began to think they sounded like the step-sisters in *Cinderella.*

Simone tossed her head to keep the tears from coming and told herself they were jealous; they had both married businessmen—wealthy businessmen, it was true, but businessmen nevertheless. Their taunts only made Simone more determined. She began to spend long afternoons in the university's music library listening to Berlioz, Bach, Wagner, and Mahler. She read *The Birth of Tragedy,* she visited the theaters where the Klimt murals were hung, she found articles on Dreyfus and Herzl so she would understand some of Arthur's allusions when they met at the Cafe Schwartzenburg and had tea, or when they went to concerts and the opera, as they were beginning to do.

Arthur was as taken with the young woman as she was with him. Simone was a handsome, tall brunette, with a stately carriage and a curious mind. She had an unusual confidence for someone so young—perhaps it came with her height—and when they were together she made him feel as if he were the only man in Vienna, perhaps in the world. And not because he had a growing reputation or because he had been left a fortune by his parents—he was an only child—or because he had read so many books. No, Simone seemed to love him only for himself, for the way he thought, for the physical characteristics he had merely accepted: his reddish hair, his gray-blue eyes, his somewhat stocky build. He had never felt like that with a woman before. When she took his arm and they walked down the aisle to their seats, Arthur Hurwitz considered himself the luckiest man in the world.

After Gertrude and Clara realized that this eminent doctor was falling in love with their baby sister, they made it their business to find out how old Arthur was. When they did, they were aghast.

"What will you do when he gets sick?"

"How will you, of all people—why, you practically faint at the sight of blood—take care of an invalid?"

And then, the cruelest of all: "What will you do when you're widowed at fifty?" they screamed to their sister whom they loved as much as they loved their children. "What will you do when you're left alone with a bunch of kids?"

But it was too late. Simone and Arthur were deeply in love and already making plans to marry. So, of course, the sisters reneged. How can you convince someone older than you not to marry your youngest sister? And Simone's parents were actually pleased, for the Hurwitz family was an old one in Vienna; though World War I had just begun they made their last child an elegant, sumptuous wedding.

Gertrude and Clara had to eat their words. Arthur was an exemplary husband, a thoughtful, intelligent man who adored Simone, who understood her needs and moods and even her stubbornness, and who was a fine father to two extraordinarily beautiful and gifted children: Leo and Lise. And because of his age, he was allowed to stay in Vienna and practice medicine during the war. Clearly, they had been wrong, they admitted to themselves as they watched Arthur's practice prosper and the children grow and Simone mature into one of the loveliest young matrons in the city.

Now, though, they were at it again. Obviously, they

had jumped to conclusions too soon. Arthur was, as they had suspected, as pigheaded as he was intelligent. For now he was insisting on taking Simone and the children away from them—to America. And why? It was so absurd as to be laughable. Because of that bumpkin, Hitler, and his brown shirts.

Who was Hitler? A crazy man with a dream, but basically small potatoes who would never amount to anything. How could a man as sophisticated as Arthur be so afraid of such a person? It was beyond them, and it was just this kind of irrational panic that encouraged such misfits as Hitler. No one in his right mind could take such a lowlife seriously. Yet Arthur did. And worse, he had somehow convinced the great and elderly Ernest Wahrhaftig to leave, too. Wahrhaftig was far too old to leave—why, he had heart trouble, only last spring he had fallen because of chest pains and still walked with a cane. Surely Arthur was insane to think of putting that old weak heart through such a traumatic displacement. Wahrhaftig and his wife should stay; Vienna was their home, where they were destined to live until they died. It was a shame, a crying shame for them to leave, for anyone to leave.

Their pleas fell on deaf ears. The Hurwitz family was leaving, Arthur had told the children when they were on holiday in Pertisau, and now the house was in a flurry of excitement and tears as Bertha and Gertrude and Clara supervised the packing and the sale of the furniture and the wonderful old house that Arthur had inherited and then altered to meet his needs.

"Never, never in a million years will they find a house like this one," Gertrude, the more outspoken one, said loudly. And then, because she and her husband had visited New York right before the Crash, she added, "They will probably have to live in some dismal flat near one of those elevateds, with the noise pounding in their ears day and night."

Even when Simone said that Arthur had threatened to ask her to leave because she was frightening Leo and Lise, Gertrude went on and on, in a whisper now, but still she couldn't stop. As she helped Bertha pack Arthur's books, as she marveled at the extensive library he had so lovingly assembled, Gertrude was convinced that her brother-in-law had lost his mind.

But, oh, how she loved Simone and the children! So she persuaded her husband and Clara and her husband that the least they could do was manufacture a business trip to Zurich and thus travel that far with the Hurwitz family.

Now they were standing at the Zurich railroad station. They had spent two days on holiday here, the eight of them, or at least Gertrude and Clara had pretended it was a holiday. They had gone to the amusement park and the two best restaurants and had bought Lise and Leo new watches, and finally, it was time to board the train for Paris. There Arthur and Simone and the children would see the Wahrhaftigs before the professor and his wife went to Edinburgh where the old man had been given a prestigious and well-paying chair. And then the Hurwitzes would go on to Rotterdam to board their ship to America.

Like all railroad stations, this one resembled a cave, and Lise felt very small as they walked from the main area to the long platforms between the tracks. It was night, and the condensing steam made odd patterns on the outsides of the railroad cars. The whole place seemed wet, perhaps because of all the weeping that had already begun.

Their train was on its track when they arrived, but as they were saying goodbye, the bow on Lise's new blouse came undone, and now Aunt Gertrude was bending toward her trying to tie the tails of the bow in her special, reliable way. But Gertrude's hands were trembling so much she couldn't make the knot, and the bow kept falling apart as she stood there, crying, holding the two tails as if she had no idea what in the world to do with them. Just as Clara was about to rescue her sister, Gertrude straightened and pursed her lips into a brave narrow smile and tied the bow. Someone looking at her from afar might have thought she was performing a task that required enormous strength.

Lise could hardly bear to look into her aunt's brimming eyes, for once she saw that sadness she knew she would start to cry, too. How awful this was! She and Leo and Papa anticipating this trip with so much pleasure, and Mama and her aunts and uncles crying those "contagious tears," as Papa called them. They were behaving as if it were the end of the world. And Mama saying they were going to America only for a visit. Even Lise knew that couldn't be true. You don't pack and ship more than two thousand books just for a visit. Surely Mama knew that.

So Lise stood there for what seemed a century and let Aunt Gertrude tie the bow properly. Then she let herself be lifted into her aunt's arms and kissed over and over again by all four of them. Such hard, rough kisses. She felt as if her face were being scorched.

At last they put her down. But when the conductor started calling, "All aboard, all aboard," Lise was still clutching her aunt's sleeve, clutching so hard she wasn't sure she could ever let go, and for weeks and months after she was eased away from Aunt Gertrude, Lise could feel the fine wool crepe of Gertrude's navy suit beneath her fingers.

America, 1931–1937

1

"Boston," Mama would say and give all her arguments in favor of that city, mostly that they had cousins named Loomis who lived there and that it had a great symphony.

"But what about Philadelphia?" Papa would invariably reply, and then give his reasons why the City of Brotherly Love might be a better choice; after all, two spinster sisters who were related to his father lived there, and it also had a great symphony.

Lise listened to them almost every evening, but she knew it was a game, for she had seen her father's eyes when he studied the map of the American Northeast. He had hung it in the tiny cabin of the *Staatendam* the first day of their trip. By the end of the voyage he seemed mesmerized by the blue line that so prominently joined New York City and Albany, the blue line that was the Hudson River. And when her father said, in his tenderest voice, "You know, Simone, Baedeker preferred the Hudson to the Rhine," Lise knew that they would at least give New York a try.

The actual city was out: too much noise, too many

people, too many doctors. But north of the city—on the Hudson—that was where Arthur Hurwitz wanted to look.

Each morning, after they had eaten a huge breakfast at the Brevoort, they would hurry to Grand Central Station and catch the train that stopped at a succession of small villages on the eastern bank of the Hudson, sleepy little villages that seemed to have escaped the sweep of world events. Here no one had heard of Hitler; here no one looked hungry or threadbare; here most of the houses—even those shingled with new asbestos instead of clapboard—were kept in decent repair. Streets were tidy, flanked by elms and maples and beeches; flower gardens still bloomed with chrysanthemum and St. John's fire at the end of October. Doors were left open, money for the milkman and the newsboy were set out in snowy envelopes under welcome mats, middle-aged couples took their exercise along the aqueduct road that started at Croton, young mothers thought nothing of leaving their babies in carriages outside the stores while they did their shopping, and the children never thought to bring in their bicycles from the lawns that stretched, like contented laps of green, before the comfortable homes.

The schools were small, but good; the populations were growing; and doctors were scarce. "There's one in Bell's Ferry, a woman," the broker told them, "but she's about to limit her practice. And a man in Appleby, but no one in Honeywell." So they decided to concentrate on Honeywell, but the house had to have a view of the river and enough room for an office for Dr. Hurwitz.

In the evenings, while they lingered over coffee, pretending they were here in this elegant art deco dining room on holiday, no different from the Germans and French and Swiss who were chatting around them, Simone's fingers would creep across the table until Arthur closed his palm over them. Tonight the children asked to be excused a little early. After they were in bed Lise whispered into the pool of light that separated them, "Leo, can we afford this?"

"Papa wouldn't do it if we couldn't afford it. He isn't stupid, you know."

"I never said he was!" Exasperated, she pulled the pillow over her head and tried to go to sleep. They were eating too much in that fancy restaurant downstairs; her parents wore their public faces all the time; she never had the energy to read before she went to sleep; and she hated wearing the dark clothes her mother insisted on each morning. Oh, to stop living in this hotel—oh, to stop being battered by the sounds of strangers! It seemed to Lise a play without an end.

On top of that she was beginning to doubt Papa, and when she finally fell asleep, all she heard in her wild, speeded-up dreams were her aunts and uncles criticizing and berating him. She didn't know which was worse—her lassitude when she was awake or those awful, accusatory dreams.

One afternoon they were trudging back to the station in air as thick as flour. A shawl of fog had thrown itself over the bank of the river. Instead of taking their usual, somewhat steep, shortcut, the Hurwitz family was walking down the main street of the town. Soon they were passing an old Victorian house. Arthur pressed his wife's arm. In front of them was the closest thing to a gingerbread house Lise had ever seen, a dismal gray-brown gingerbread house. But it had twin turrets and a wide apron of a porch and some ziggedy-zaggedy windows that surely overlooked the river. And it sat contentedly, not minding its shabbiness in the least, like someone stuffed from a huge dinner.

"Who owns it?" her father asked.

"Oh, an old widow with plenty of money. A real miser. Never has it painted." The broker's voice was melancholy. "And look at that grass. Won't even water it, that one."

"Would she be interested in selling?" Papa asked. Her mother gave an audible gasp. Even through the fog Lise could see the broker's amazement.

"Are you serious?"

"Absolutely."

Then the four of them hurried down the hill for their train. The railroad ran along the river, but today they could barely see the water.

Lise leaned into the woven raffia seat and felt a loose strand of straw dig into her back. Yet she welcomed the pain. It kept her awake. Then she could hear what they were saying. French phrases flitted around her ears. Alert now, she waited to hear that they would be poor. Instead her mother sighed, "What a fool I was to complain when you insisted on putting that money away. I can't believe I was such a fool." Then her father's murmur. Though she couldn't hear his words, Lise knew, from the timbre of his voice, that he was probably smiling and patting her mother's gloved hand.

Finally, Lise let herself relax. She could feel her brain shutting out everything but the rhythmic clacking of the train as it wound its way back to New York. When they arrived at Grand Central, Simone tried to wash Lise's face, but she soon realized that the smudgy rings under the child's eyes weren't soot, as she had thought.

"She exhausted!" Mama's voice was trembling. Lise was confused as she looked from one parent to the other, but no one protested when it was decided that they take a holiday the next day.

In perfect Indian summer weather, the Hurwitz family wandered through Central Park, then browsed through bookstores and antique shops. They felt like contented tourists. Before it was time to go back to the hotel, they stopped to buy a potted chrysanthemum. That was what brought them luck, Mama insisted. For when they returned a message awaited them: "The widow has decided she can go to live with one of her children."

And that night Leo and Lise were allowed to have champagne with dinner.

2

The Hudson made the Aachen See look like a pond. At the beginning of twilight, at that brink in the day when light and dark are in balance, a blackness seemed to grow from the huge expanse of water, and an endless baggy cloak of rising darkness, as vague as mist, seemed to meet the dimming light that was descending slowly from the sky. Its beauty was eerie, especially during that first winter, when dusk would tumble down so quickly; then Lise felt as if she were hanging in limbo: nowhere and anywhere. She would stand at her window staring at those extravagant sunsets and imagine herself on some peak in the Karwendel, for by now the streets were quiet and the shopkeepers would be pulling in their awnings and going upstairs to their dinners. The rooftops that extended below their house on Main Street could easily be taken for mountains, and if she squinted a little she could be back in Austria.

Yet Europe was receding in her mind, and now, when letters from her aunts arrived, referring to Hitler as an "ill wind that will blow away" or implying that Papa was "making a mountain out of a molehill," Lise would watch her parents grow awkward with each other, avert their eyes, almost avoid each other for a day or sometimes more. So after a while her heart would sink when she saw those letters addressed in her aunts' spidery hands. Leave us alone, part of her would say, while the other part could hardly wait to read the news from Vienna and then go up to her room where she would answer Gertrude's and Clara's meticulously detailed questions.

One day, almost a year after they moved to Honeywell, Arthur Hurwitz announced that he was going to witness Tashlik from the newly completed George Washington Bridge. Simone refused—too much to do. Rosh Hashanah was a few days away. "But take the children, it will be interesting," she said.

Lise enjoyed these forays into religion here in America. Back in Vienna they had celebrated the Jewish holidays with exhausting, marathon dinners at Gertrude's, but here they went to a Reform temple in Appleby and her parents seemed much more interested in the rituals and all the other aspects of Judaism. And she and Leo went to religious school for the first time in their lives.

"Tashlik is an ancient ceremony during which Jews all over the world find a flowing body of water—usually a river—into which they can throw their sins before entering a synagogue for the New Year," her father explained as they went south on the train. "For only if they are cleansed can they pray to be inscribed in the Book of Life for the coming year. What we'll be seeing is the Orthodox community of Washington Heights performing Tashlik."

A razor-sharp wind cut through the raucously blue sky. Lise hugged her heavy sweater tighter, amazed that hundreds of men were standing on the bridge dressed in suits and tallits and yarmulkas, apparently oblivious to the sudden change of weather. Their tallits luffed like sails around their bodies; from a distance it was as if all the sails in the Aachen See through all the summers of her childhood had come together on this bridge thousands and thousands of miles away. From this height the Hudson was blue-black and looked far larger than it ever seemed when you were walking along it. Its scale seemed to have expanded to match the monstrous bridge that now spanned it.

Lise stared below her. The height made her dizzy. With the unfamiliar hum of the prayers and this great surge of humanity swaying as it prayed, she seemed to have been transported to another world. She imagined the sins as curling, leechlike creatures—meeting and bumping in the brackish waters below. For here, the tidal water of the Atlantic Ocean mixed with the downward fresh flow of the river so that it was a river that ran in two directions. And now, into that incessant conflict of salt and fresh water came sins, as well. What a mysterious Hudson this was! Yet now she could understand why it was so important to these religious Jews. Only in the Hudson could sins be washed into the Atlantic and truly disappear. What better way to be cleansed?

When they arrived home, her father seemed different, although he had not participated in the praying. His face was triumphant, younger, as he told his wife, "It was beautiful—all of them praying, no one bothering or mocking them, everyone free to do as he wished. Wonderful." This is a country where we can live in peace, his eyes told his wife and children. This is a country where we will all be safe, his eyes said, as they would on all the succeeding holidays of his life.

It was only later, years later, when Lise knew it wasn't

going to be as simple as Papa had thought, that she suddenly wondered how in the world those yarmulkas had stayed on all those heads in that fierce, raw wind.

3

The house exceeded Simone Hurwitz's worst fears: rotting sills, broken sashes, warped floors, stopped-up pipes, and gossamer curtains of web and dust hanging from every corner. Yet its spaces were gracious and airy, there were three fireplaces with wide stone hearths, two bay windows, those twin turrets that had first caught Arthur's eye, and plenty of rooms in which to put up relatives and friends, maybe even her beloved, foolish sisters.

For the first few months the family lived only on the first floor: Simone and Arthur in the dining room, which was on the right of the large center hall, and Lise and Leo in the living room on the left. The children slept at either end of the long couch that was the only thing Simone had bought from the miserly widow, and each evening she would make it up with the eiderdowns from Vienna.

Those eiderdowns, covered in a sturdy rose-colored cotton, had been the bane of Arthur's life when they were packing, but now here they were, covering the children—warming them, comforting them as they dreamed their way into sleep, their beautiful features lit by the glow of the fire that flickered like a pulse in that large unfamiliar room. Gertrude and Clara had been right.

"At least you will have these," they had insisted as they folded and punched the huge quilts down into the boxes, determined not to buckle under Arthur's disapproving looks. Of course, he had thought it utter folly to take such bulky items to America. But they had been made for their grandmother by a famous quiltmaker in Vienna and were still as good as new: not a sign on them of all the people who had slept under them, not a stain from the occasional nosebleed or heavy menstrual flow or small child's accident. Nothing. And what would it cost to replace such quilts, which were as light as a feather yet as warm as toast? Gertrude and Clara wanted to know. No, Simone was not going to America without them, they decided as they punched and pushed and finally made the marvelous old quilts fit into the paltry boxes Arthur had provided.

For once Lise was glad Papa had been overruled, for she loved the voluminous lightness of her eiderdown. You didn't just fall asleep, you floated asleep under it. And invariably slept well. It seemed like a command.

Simone did an incredible job of fixing up that wreck of a white elephant, and by their first Passover in the house the wood floors glowed, there were flowered rugs in the most important rooms, the furniture she had found across the river in Nyack had been refinished, and curtains hung at every window. Then Simone began working on the garden, for she had decided in the first moment she saw the house that the dull, burned-out lawn would become a colorful mass of flowers. When their cousins from Boston and Philadelphia arrived for the holiday, they exclaimed that the house looked as if the family had been living there for years. The outside was now painted a deep slate blue—a Hudson blue, Arthur called it—with a white trim. And Arthur's office was soon fully equipped, although he had to wait to use it until he passed his licensing examination. In the meantime, he worked at a nearby hospital. But the people in Honeywell knew he was a trained doctor and were already coming to ask his advice.. In return they would leave packages of food or plants on the front porch, or send their children to shovel snow. And one morning a neighbor presented Simone with an experimental shower head that became the delight of her life.

By the second May in the house the garden was as lovely as a well-planned room: rosebeds and box on the outside and the bulb and perennial beds in the middle. A man from the local newspaper came to take pictures, and when Cousin Sally Loomis from Boston came to Honeywell, she demanded, "And when did she have time to plant those hyacinths and daffodils?"

"Oh, she and Lise did that the first weekend we actually owned the house," Arthur replied. "The first year they weren't as showy, but now they are beginning to divide." Hearing him and Sally talk, Lise was astonished. It seemed a lifetime since that day only a year and a half ago when Mama's hair had been blowing wildly in the November wind as she cried, "Toss the bulbs, Liselotte, and we'll plant them where they fall!" How frightened she had been then, Lise remembered. But not Mama. No, her mother was determined to have the prettiest garden she could, and it was not for her to plant tame circles of bulbs like the sedate ladies of Honeywell's garden club. No, it would have to be more dramatic and spectacular for Simone Hurwitz. And, of course, it was. Yet how like Papa to give her mother and Lise all the credit when he and Leo had done all the heavy work.

Her mother's passion for gardening was new. In Vienna she had been content to let an old family retainer do the planting and weeding, but by their second year in

Honeywell she threw herself into the sheer physical work with astounding energy. Lise was too young to see it for what it was, yet when Arthur observed his wife he knew that she was assuaging her anger—at him? at her sisters? at Hitler? he sometimes didn't know which—by creating this gorgeous garden. He also knew that when Simone loved a plant, she had to have it. Even when it was against the law to dig up wild flowers in New York State.

Of course, they weren't looking for it. They had been walking along the eastern bank of the Hudson searching for mushrooms and had reached that spot about ten miles north of Honeywell where the river flanges out into the shape of a plate, what the Dutch named the Tappan Zee.

Lise and her father had dropped behind. Now Papa was explaining that a glacial cut in the floor of the Atlantic gave the river its tidal flow almost to Poughkeepsie, where it then met the downward flow of the river from Lake Tear of the Clouds, which was hundreds of miles away in the Adirondacks. "Poughkeepsie is a crucial point, the Indians named it and it means 'safe harbor,'" he said. "They also called the river the Mukkeakunnuk, which means the river that flows two ways." They walked a little farther. "When I was in Vienna I felt like this river, always going in two directions, pulled to stay and pulled to leave. But now it's better."

Lise was surprised to hear her father say that; he so rarely expressed his feelings. And he wasn't finished. "Many people live in that suspended state all their lives, but perhaps it's easier for them to fool themselves, be just slightly dishonest with themselves. But it's wrong. One must be truthful with oneself and with others, it's the only way." She stared, and when she looked into his gray eyes— her eyes, everyone said—she expected them to be solemn.

But no, the moral lesson was over and now he was reaching for her hand. Together they clambered over the steeper rocks to where Mama and Leo were sitting.

Leo was bored, he hadn't wanted to come on this walk, he would have preferred to be with his friends, he was too old for these Sunday hikes with his parents, he had muttered to Lise when they were getting ready. But Mama's eyes were oblivious to Leo's discomfort, oblivious to anything but a small blossom that had sprouted among the roots of the maples. A floppy wild flower that looked part cyclamen, part violet, but was pale yellow with other light markings near its edge.

"What's that?" Papa asked.

"I have no idea, I've never seen it before," her mother replied.

"It must be native, look, there are hundreds." Yet when they walked about twenty feet north the flower had disappeared. Nor were there any more for the rest of the day.

Mama was stymied. Arriving home from school, Lise and Leo would find her hunched over her gardening books. How frustrating it was! "It's nowhere, nothing with those odd colors or spoon-shaped leaves." Finally she went to the Honeywell garden club.

"That looks like wild pansy," one woman exclaimed when she saw Leo's drawing. "It blooms with the late violets and looks like one. Sometimes you see it into summer, it's native to the west coast, California and Oregon, but I've never seen it around here. We used to call it 'hearts-ease.' "

Hearts-ease. How perfect. She had to have some, Simone decided. The following May she picked Lise up from school early and they took a train north, trudging along the trail to where she hoped to find the patch of laurel she had marked on the map. To the east of that was the hearts-ease.

Lise would never forget her mother's face when she spied the carpet of flowers swaying lightly against the twisted roots. "Oh, darling, I knew we'd find them!" she said, though she had been murmuring all along the way, "I hope all that terrible cold last winter didn't kill them."

Now they sat down and rewarded themselves with the pears that had been weighing down Lise's pocket for the last hour. Craning their necks so the juice wouldn't drip on their clothes, they slowly, languorously bit into the fruit. After she had finished and wiped her lips with her white hankie, her mother smiled. Lise had never seen her so content, except maybe on their holidays in Pertisau. But not the last time; then her mother had reminded her of a finch at the bird feeder, constantly worried that its nibbling would be cut short by a rude, noisy jay. And her father's mouth set in that straight, unsmiling seam. Yet all that was past, thank goodness, and Mama was saying, again, "Aren't we lucky to have found them?" Lise nodded. The air was syrup, her eyelids lead.

When she awoke, her head was in Mama's lap. The damp smell of her mother's skin enclosed Lise in its sweetness, and Mama's gray cotton skirt was limp against Lise's cheek, soothing in its softness, so unlike its starched self that hung so smartly in her mother's closet. So soft and soothing Lise would have dropped off again, if not for a faint, breathy whistle that filled the air. Mama was fast asleep. Lise lay there as still as she could, utterly content, under the umbrella of sprouting leaves above her head. But when she turned her wrist to see the time, she was filled with panic. After five! Papa would be frantic, they hadn't told him where they were going.

Quickly Lise rose and shook her mother's shoulder. Mama's eyelids fluttered open, the pupils a deep, brownish black that had not a trace of worry in them. So different from those eyes when they looked at her and Leo and Papa, or even at the furniture and rugs.

Although they had to hurry, they smoothed the damp brown earth over the holes. "They'll fill in," her mother said. "But, darling, not a word."

"What will you say if someone asks about them?"

"I'll say they found us."

4

The Hudson didn't disappoint Arthur Hurwitz. It became his pastime, his hobby—indeed, his obsession. In addition to his notebook titled *Europe* in which he recorded his anguish over the progress of events there, he had another notebook that he called *The Hudson.* In it he gathered facts, his impressions, legends about the river.

Within a year after he had hung that smartly lettered shingle, which Leo had painted, on the front gate, Arthur Hurwitz had a busy practice. In the high-ceilinged dining room that doubled as his waiting room and was filled with flowers from his wife's fabulous garden, the wealthier families, who lived east of Main Street and could trace their ancestry to the tenant farmers of the Van Cortlandts and Philipses and Van Rensselaers, would mingle with the shopkeepers and blue-collar workers whose families had come to Honeywell in the late nineteenth century from Italy and Ireland. Soon people began to notice that the room was lined with books about Hudson and the river and the valley: James Fenimore Cooper, Washington Irving, Carl Carmer. When the schoolchildren had to construct balsa wood villages of the early colonies, they would ask Dr. Hurwitz for pictures and maps and would be rewarded, if the doctor had time, with a tale about Rip Van Winkle or Ichabod Crane, or the less well-known Rambout Van Dam, a young buck whose spirit was still said to be wandering around the Tappan Zee because he had foolishly tried to row across the river in the early hours of a Sunday morning after staying out late at a party. For the sin of breaking the Sabbath, his ghost was condemned to sail forever on that tiny sea.

"Arthur is becoming an authority on the Hudson," Simone would write to her sisters. Before long Arthur could recount the entire story of Hudson's landing, the sweet smell that floated from the river and its banks and overwhelmed the early explorers.

"Imagine the smell of a thousand lilacs, an explosion of lilacs, more than you could ever find in one place," he would begin, so that all those listening could almost feel the fragrance filling their nostrils, a fragrance so remarkable that every man who explored the Hudson River recorded it in his log.

By the time Lise was in high school, her father had made it a habit to take students each spring to the spot where the steamship, the *Henry Clay,* burned in the worst disaster on the river.

"It is a lesson in stubbornness," he always began. They would be standing on a little point north of Yonkers. "A man named Collyer had had to sell one steamboat, the *Armenia,* to get enough money to finish a larger one, the *Henry Clay.* When the *Henry Clay* was completed it cost $38,000 and was 206 feet long. One July day in 1852, both ships were making the trip from Albany to New York, and as the men hawked tickets, each bragged that his boat was the faster. So, before the ships had left the wharf, a race was on.

"Collyer was a foolish, selfish man. He ordered his crew to tie down the safety valves in the boiler and then began to taunt the crew of the *Armenia*. The pilot of the *Henry Clay* reminded Collyer that racing in the Hudson was against the law, but Collyer wouldn't listen. And the captain was sick in his cabin with food poisoning. Collyer was in command. When he caught up with the *Armenia,* the guardrails of the boats locked; the *Armenia* slowed down and floated free, and for a moment, that looked like the end of the race. But Collyer urged his crew to go faster, ordering them to keep the safety valves tied down. Some frightened passengers insisted on getting off at Poughkeepsie, and there, the crew begged Collyer to stop. He refused and ordered them to continue at full speed though the *Armenia* was far behind. But here—" her father would stop and point to the place on the map he was holding, "here the *Henry Clay* caught fire. The pilot begged Collyer to beach her, but Collyer merely stood at the helm staring straight ahead. Finally, the pilot brought the burning boat ashore. Some of the passengers tried to swim to safety. But people often didn't know how to swim in those days, and this river is full of unexpected tides. Seventy-two people died, including Maria Hawthorne, Nathaniel's sister; Andrew Jackson Downing, the great landscape architect; and Stephen Allen, who was once mayor of New York City."

Here he would stop and draw a long breath. "Collyer and his crew were acquitted. It seems amazing that that could happen, doesn't it?" He would raise his thick eyebrows at those listening students, then continue, "But less than a year later the state legislature passed the Steamboat Inspection Act, which put an end to any illegal racing on the Hudson."

Now that Lise read the papers every day, she knew why her father needed to tell this story, why he gave up a day in his office to do it, and why he didn't seem to notice that he was standing in a hot sun or a cold drizzle as he told it.

It was a quiet life they led in Honeywell: the doctor's practice, the relatives from Boston and Philadelphia, the friends who were coming from Europe and the ones they made here. Lise and Leo never felt strange, although they were among the very small minority of Jewish students in the schools; and here the year was punctuated, as it had never been in Vienna, by the Jewish holidays. At temple and Sunday school she and Leo met people who were to be their friends for life—like the Hubers—and her parents went to meetings and breakfasts and coffees. Often they would come home looking drained and defeated, and then Lise would know that the discussions had not been about more money for the projected temple building but had involved plans and schemes for getting more Jews out of Austria and Germany.

For the letters from Vienna had changed. Nothing was ever said about the political situation, Hitler's name was never mentioned anymore, and there was a resigned tiredness that seemed to seep through the words, even in the letters to Lise and Leo. Reading those letters made Lise sad, and when she passed them on to her mother, she would lower her eyes and soon make some excuse to go to her room. The last thing she wanted was to see Mama cry.

Papa had been right. Yet while the new settlers—the refugees—were scurrying around trying to find homes and jobs, the Hurwitzes had everything they could want: her mother's garden, this wonderful spacious house, good schools. And music. Whatever the season, music floated through the house. There were concerts and museums in New York, and each spring and fall an excursion to the Botanical Garden where Mama would fly, paper and pencil in hand, through one greenhouse after another.

Best were the occasional trips to the Metropolitan Opera. Then her mother would wear those lush blue or brown velvet suits from Vienna, those old-fashioned clothes made before anyone was worrying about Hitler, with skirts skimming the red carpeting of the old opera house and with a softness matching the worn, sometimes threadbare seats. Lise loved those trips, which began with *Hansel and Gretel* the first Christmas after they arrived, and though it sometimes embarrassed her as she grew older, she understood why her parents hated to leave and lingered in their seats after the end of the performance and after the rest of the audience had long since gone. It was a little bit of Europe right here in New York.

And flowing through their new life was this extraordinary river: sometimes a magnificent slab of burnished bronze, sometimes a torrent of whitecaps, occasionally a tightly woven blanket motionless beneath a slaty fog, once in a great while a sheet of milky glass supporting brightly scarved skaters. But what Lise loved most of all were those wildly thunderous summer nights. Clad in rubber boots and ponchos, she and Leo and Papa would stand on the bank of the river, shuddering as each diamond streak of lightning seared the blackness that was air and water combined. And when they turned to go back home, there was that speck of light shining bravely from her parents' room where Mama would be knitting or reading, counting the minutes until they returned.

Graduation, 1938

1

The day couldn't have been more promising. It began for Lise when a whisper of breeze billowed her curtain until the filmy whiteness brushing her cheek woke her. Within seconds she heard, "How lucky we are!" The climber had bloomed. From that thorny maze of green—roses!

Lise smiled at the sound of such sheer joy surging upward. Then she heard Leo's voice, so much deeper since he had gone to college, and the high horselaugh of Cousin Sally who had insisted on coming though she was recently widowed, and the tinkling, ceaseless sounds drifting from the kitchen where dishes and glasses and silver were being unwrapped and washed and placed on trays.

Her mother had invited the entire graduating class with their parents this afternoon at four o'clock. After a week of cool, steady drizzle, the sky had cleared and was now a blinding blue. Lise threw back the covers and stepped onto the old wood floor. When she caught sight of herself in the full-length mirror, she ran her fingers through her hair. It tumbled loose in the light. Not as red now as when they first came to Honeywell, but still startling hair. Quickly she ran a brush through it and gathered it into a loose ponytail; then she slipped on her robe.

"No slippers?" Mama asked, then held her face sideways for Lise's kiss.

"Too hot. Isn't it a gorgeous day?" Mother and daughter exchanged a conspiratorial glance. They had never discussed what they would do if it rained, and now they were as giddy as two inexperienced gamblers on a winning streak.

Graduation was scheduled for two o'clock. Several students had been chosen to play musical selections. Lise wanted to run through the Mendelssohn Fantasy again, help her mother, then shower and dress. She ate quickly and went upstairs and pulled on a skirt and blouse and tidied her room.

On her way downstairs, she bumped into her father. He had canceled his office hours and was using the time to fix doorknobs, hang pictures, prop a weary bookcase. So rarely did she see him with a hammer in his hand that the sight of it made her laugh. He raised an eyebrow.

"You look so fierce," she explained.

"Where are you off to in such a hurry?"

"I have to run through the Mendelssohn."

"In that case, I'll fix the bookcase now." He followed her into the living room. Whenever he could, he would listen to her practice. Even during these last months when he had been glued to the radio and newspapers, even when his face became gray—actually gray—after the news of the *Anschluss* in March, he had listened and discussed her music with her. So different from Mama whose greatest pleasure seemed to come from watching her play.

The piece went well. Lise knew she hadn't imagined

it when she saw her father's glowing eyes. "What about the softer passages? Were they clear enough?"

"Yes, Lise, they were, the whole thing was perfect."

"Perfect! Absolutely perfect!" Her mother exulted as she hurried through the rosebed, stopping only to cut the lighter blooms, the whites and pinks and apricots that had reached their peak. "Isn't this wonderful?" Then she dropped the blossoms into the basket Sally was holding. "Be careful of thorns. The last thing Lise needs today is a thorn."

How it happened Lise didn't know, but at the end she had to rush. When she felt the smooth cotton of her graduation dress sticking to her she realized, suddenly, how hot it had become. Ninety-one, she saw on the thermometer outside her window. Yet she had to dash. Her mother's worried voice, urging her to hurry, kept bouncing up the stairs. Finally Leo boomed, "For God's sake, Lise, shake a leg!"

"All right, all right," she shouted, jabbing hairpins into her hair. Quickly she outlined her mouth with lipstick and rubbed some kohl on her eyelids. Surely in all the excitement no one would notice.

Only when she was sitting on the auditorium stage between Suzy Huber and Lawrence Inkeles did she remember her music sitting on the piano at home. "Only a fool doesn't bring his music," her teacher always said, and here she was, the biggest fool of all. How could she have forgotten? Straining, she stared into the audience, and finally she spotted her parents. Lise could see her father's gray head and beard bend again and again as he made his way toward the third row where Leo was saving seats; it was a slow journey; all his patients wanted to greet him.

At last the Pledge of Allegiance and the "Star-Spangled Banner." Then the speeches. On and on they droned. Lise's palms became sticky; she kept wiping them with her hankie and tried to make her mind a blank so she would stop worrying about her music. After all, she had played it perfectly five hours ago. Finally the speeches were over. The flute player took her place. Following her were a string ensemble, a singer, a brass quintet, then Lise. "The best for last," the principal had whispered to her yesterday.

Relax, try to relax, she told herself as she waited for two boys to move the piano to the middle of the stage. One of them smiled. Encouraged, Lise conjured up her father's face after she had played this morning.

She sat down, then moved from side to side on the bench, as she always did before she played. Then she rubbed her palms together and took out her handkerchief and put it on one side of the bridge. But when she looked straight ahead, the very thing she had feared happened. She had no idea where to begin. The music had flown from her mind; even when she tried to fix its cover in her head—that creamy, slightly frayed cover with the black gothic letters—even when she could do that, no notes came.

In desperation she looked out at her parents. Her mother sat proudly, her head a little higher than usual, tilted for a better view. But her father knew. In that second when their eyes made contact, Lise saw that Papa knew. She gave what she hoped was an imperceptible shrug. Someone coughed. She moved the bench a little farther from the piano. She had heard of people forgetting in amateur situations like this, and after a moment of embarrassment, the music would be found and spread before the performer. After all, Myra Hess used music. But she was an idiot, she didn't have her music.

Oh, what was she going to do? Her glance flickered back to her father. He was frowning. Then he put his forefinger to his lips and she read "B-flat," and suddenly, thank God, there it was, whole, the first page hanging in her mind. She began, and with each measure the music got stronger, more assured. She could feel that she was playing well, yet she felt as if she were moving in a dream. None of it—her fingers, the keys, the sounds—seemed real. She was breathless and drenched with sweat when it was over.

Afterward, Lise wanted to explain to her father what had happened, but he waved away her doubts and insisted, "It was wonderful."

"But I didn't even feel I was playing. Someone else seemed to be guiding my fingers and feet. It was eerie," she told him. He shook his head; he would have none of it. "It was wonderful, whoever was playing. I only hope Mendelssohn was listening." His praise only made her feel worse.

"What talent!" "I hope she'll continue with her music." "Is she interested in a musical career?" "An angel, she played like an angel," people said. Lise felt strange, false. Frightened. Yet she inched through the smiling throng, accepting their lavish compliments, for she didn't know what else to do. But later she made a silent vow—to play only for herself.

The party was a huge success: women in flowing pastel dresses swirling on their husbands' arms; radiant girls in white pirouetting through the crowd; diffident boys with slicked-down hair and scrubbed faces standing at the edges until they could no longer resist the punch and tea sandwiches and cookies and cake. The murmurous hum of voices rising and falling as everyone relaxed and began to drink and eat. Simone's roses swaying tipsily in their bowls as people stopped to touch them, amazed that they were real. Spongy, cool grass under the soles. The sky deepening from blue to mauve. And then, after everyone had eaten, the sound of feet rushing up the stairs as Lise's classmates tumbled from one turret to the other, fascinated by the gracious house.

Just when she was beginning to enjoy herself, when that eerie feeling after she had played was beginning to dissolve, the guests began to say goodbye. As she sank into a chair, Lise felt hollow. Now, tired rinds of fruit lay at the bottom of the glasses and bowls. Voices were lowered, as if in mourning. Into the silence came the *snap! snap!* of the chairs as Leo and Mr. Morgan, the handyman, folded them and stacked them.

"Come, darling, we need your chair," her mother urged as she hurried past. Now that the party was over, Mama seemed bent on removing all vestiges of it. Why couldn't they leave it alone? Lise wondered. Why couldn't they stop and sit here and let the sounds of all the people and the combined fragrance of the food and roses and coffee and the river linger in the air? Why were grownups so anxious to get on to the next thing? Slowly she dragged herself into the kitchen.

"You're as pale as that wall behind you. You'd better sit down," Gina said. Gina was the wife of the man who owned the fish store in Honeywell, and she helped in the kitchen whenever the Hurwitz family had a party. Gratefully, Lise let herself be bullied by this woman she barely knew, this woman who seemed to be the only one here who had any idea how she felt.

"Hot drinks are better than cold in this weather,"

Gina began to say, as she handed Lise the tea, then turned, and Lise heard, "Oh, no!" and saw a flash of badge on a dark blue uniform of the new young policeman, James Mulcahy, and then " . . . a stillborn . . . his wife gave birth to a stillborn . . . such a shame . . ." as an oversize piece of cake was cut boldly from what was left and pricked with toothpicks and carefully wrapped in waxed paper.

Soon all was quiet again until the kitchen was spotless. Then her mother appeared with a fistful of bills. Still Lise sat. Only when her father passed through and gave her an inquiring look did she rise: She felt like a sleepwalker as she made her way through the dining room and up the stairs. She thought: The whole thing might not have happened, the whole thing could have been a dream.

When she passed her parents' room, Lise saw that her mother was asleep. But her father was hunched over the radio, listening to the news. Since the *Anschluss* not a day—not even her graduation day—went by when he didn't listen to the evening news. Lise wished she could say or do something to relieve his constant worry about Europe. But what was there to say?

2

The house was dead quiet. Everyone was taking a nap before dinner. Lise stirred lightly in her slip. How hot it still was! The breeze had died, and now it was suffocating. Ever since she was a child she had found it difficult to breathe in this river heat. But if she tried to read, the mosquitoes would eat her alive. So she lay there, thinking, dozing. Suddenly a light was blinding her.

"Stop that!" she cried. "You know I hate that." Leo was standing in the doorway holding a flashlight.

"Sorry. But it's still the fastest way to wake you." He was wearing a T-shirt and holding a towel.

"I was up, but I must have dropped off again. Anyone else up?"

"No, not a sound except Sally snoring. How about a swim?"

"Oh, Leo, should we?" The question was almost a reflex. Although they had been forbidden to swim in the Hudson since they were children, they had begun to do it when they were teenagers. Yet tonight it seemed wrong to disobey their parents, who had made her such an elaborate party and who were peacefully sleeping, never suspecting a thing.

"Sure we should. We've been doing it for years. It's perfectly safe."

They had begun to swim in the Hudson when Leo started to smoke; he was sixteen and she was thirteen. They would go down to the small park near the river where all the other teenagers went to smoke on the sly. On hot summer nights half the high school would be in the water. Soon, on those stifling nights when the two fans in the living room didn't seem to be moving a breath of air, Lise and Leo would pretend they were going for a walk and take a swim instead. Gliding through the cool black water, Lise never felt that she was doing anything wrong. Yes, there were tides, but no waves or undertow. The swimming was as easy as it looked. The water just buoyed her up and let her float, and the sounds around her were whispers, water murmurs lulling her into calmness, coolness. She always felt guilty when they returned, but no one even seemed to notice. Her parents would be exactly where they had left them: Mama sewing or reading in her chair, Papa reading in his.

So why should she hesitate now? Leo was right. And it was so hot. Too hot not to go. Of course she would join him. While Lise changed, Leo left a note on the kitchen table saying they had gone for a walk. Quickly they slipped out of the house. On their way to the river they saw no one, but once there they spied clusters of cigarettes sparkling like fireflies and heard splashing and laughing.

The Hudson was inky, still, and not even that cold, though it was early for swimming. Lise crawled through its smoky blackness, each stroke stronger than the last. She loved to swim in this river, perhaps because she felt, after watching it all these years, that it was hers.

"It's perfectly safe, some people swim in it," she had sometimes told her mother, testing her.

But Mama always shook her head. "I don't like even the *idea* of swimming in it, let alone doing it. There's too much going on in that river. It's as fickle as a cat."

Off in the distance a horn throbbed. Except for that insistent sound of the barge lumbering its way upriver, she and Leo and the other swimmers could have been anywhere on earth, swimming under an incredible blanket of stars that covered them like a vast sparkling cocoon. The same stars that hovered over Vienna were here, all the stars from her childhood: Arcturus, Vega, the Dragon, Regulus, Leo, the Great Bear, and the Little Bear. As she swam Lise wondered about her old friends, her cousins, and especially her aunts and uncles.

Could Papa be wrong? Could they still be in their large, luxurious houses, or had they been hounded out of them in the middle of a scary night by the Nazis? Would they ever know?

For, now the letters from her aunts merely dribbled in—sometimes taking months to arrive. And Mama's eyes were filmed almost constantly with a scrim of bewilderment that seemed to thicken with each passing week. If some kind, concerned soul ever asked after those sisters in Europe, Mama's voice had a catch in it—probably audible only to Lise and Leo and Papa, but there, nevertheless—and she would answer, with a narrow smile, "They say no news is good news." But her face would reveal what a lie that was.

Never would Lise understand it. Perfectly sane people staying in that maniac world that Europe had become when they could have gotten out and been safe here in the United States. What could have possessed them?

Back home the lights were on and everyone was up: Sally and Mama were setting food out on the kitchen table; Papa was in his office. Their mother glanced briefly at them, but she said nothing.

Suddenly Lise volunteered, "We were swimming, in the river." No more lies. That performance this afternoon felt like a lie—and that was enough. Frowning, Leo stared at her.

But Mama didn't break the rhythm of what she was doing. "I know," she told her children with a smile. "I've always known. And did you know that your father used to follow you and stand on the bank and watch you, then rush home while you dressed and manufactured excuses for your wet hair?"

Lise felt a shock of surprise go through her. All sorts of things became clear: why her parents hadn't been upset or even questioned them when they came home, why they often refused to go to visit friends on a summer evening, saying it was cooler here. And she and Leo had thought they were being so careful, toweling their hair almost dry, inventing fibs about sudden showers.

Oh, what a joke on them! All at once everyone was

laughing—wonderful, uncontrollable laughter from way down deep in their chests. Lise went to get her father.

He stood over his desk, which held the large map of Europe she had known since their arrival in Honeywell. An old, creased map with German lettering. It looked bloodstained: Germany had become a red splotch, and so had Austria. Her father was frowning as he studied it. As soon as he felt her presence, he looked up.

"And soon Czechoslovakia will be red, too. Under that idiot, Henlein, the Sudetenland is gone already, the rest is only a matter of time."

He looked so old, years older than he had this afternoon when he had whispered her music to her. Fear seized her throat. He was old. Because Mama was so young people assumed her father was younger than he actually was, but Lise knew that Papa was almost seventy. And now, instead of looking fifty-eight or sixty, he looked his real age. The lines on his face seemed to deepen while she stared at him. His face was as preoccupied as it was whenever he had to do something pressing: deliver a baby, meet someone in the emergency room, go to the police station because of an accident, or—as Lise suddenly remembered—take care of Wahrhaftig's legs.

"Come, Papa, leave this, let's go into the kitchen," she urged, putting her hand on his arm. "Mama just told us about the swimming. And all these years we were so sure we were putting something over on you." Now she felt better, the laughter was welling up inside her again.

He smiled, and his eyes brightened. Then he folded the map and placed it in the top drawer of his desk. He straightened the blotter, checked the window and shut off the light. Back in the kitchen, after they had told the story of the swimming once more, Lise looked at her parents and felt tears rising in her throat. To take such trouble for his children. How many times had he followed them? How many times had he been tired, happy to sit there and read and listen to his records, only to have to rush after them? Lise couldn't even begin to count all the nights when she and Leo had slipped out to swim, certain that no one would ever know. And when they returned, scurrying past their parents as stealthily as thieves, they could have sworn that neither of them had moved from their chairs. Oh, what a joke on them!

For the first time all day Lise was hungry. She ate slowly, thinking, How easy it is to be a child.

Soon Sally asked, "Too late for a little Chopin?" and Lise surprised herself by nodding. Anything to make Papa forget the radio and the newspapers and that brutal red stain that was spreading through Europe. Anything to make him look younger, more like the Papa she knew.

This afternoon she had been sure she would never play the piano again. She had made a silent vow, but she could never keep it. For the piano was like a magnet, a symbol of all that was good and safe about America. As long as you could make such gorgeous music, all would be right with the world. Lise sat down and placed her hands on the cool, silvery keys. This time her hands were sure and steady as—one after another—mazurkas and waltzes and impromptus ribboned their way through the high-ceilinged rooms, then flowed over the sills and doorjambs into the still-warm night. Couples latching their screen doors for the night could hear them; so could children having trouble getting to sleep because of the sudden heat. And the few swimmers who were left in the river must have lifted their heads, not quite sure what it was they heard.

Winter, 1941

She couldn't get the girl out of her room. She just sat there asking Lise more and more questions about the Brontës when the answers were right there in their notes. Of course there had to be something else on Marcia's mind. The nineteenth-century novel was merely an excuse to get into Lise's room.

They had met last spring when they were sophomores. A faint smell of shad had floated up from the river and had mixed with the sweet aura of the redbud and magnolia, the andromeda and azalea that were beginning to bloom on the Vassar campus. A circle of girls was studying on the grass, summer-warm breezes made it an idyllic day, and after a few hours the silence was broken by an exchange of small confidences, some laughter, and relief, as the conversation meandered from one thing to another and finally stopped at plans for the summer. While they were reminiscing about their childhood summers, Lise mentioned Pertisau and the Aachen See.

One of the girls suddenly narrowed her eyes and said, "Why, you have no trace of an accent. I had no idea you were a refugee."

"I'm not." Lise had been through this once before, with one of her high school teachers. She knew how a refugee was defined by Webster's—as someone who flees to safety, who has no place to go. The kind of refugee this girl meant was a person who had had to get out of Europe in the late thirties. But her family had come when there were still choices; Papa had always said they were in exile, self-imposed exile. "We banished ourselves," he once said.

"But you weren't born here, were you?"

"No, I was born in Vienna, and my family came here in 1931, when I was ten," Lise replied. "But we're not refugees."

Of course you are; what do you think we are, fools? their eyes said as they stared back at her. And Lise knew that from that moment onward they would begin to avoid her. Why, she could not fathom, for they were Jewish, too.

"It's not worth thinking about, Lise," Suzy Huber said more than once. Suzy was her childhood friend who was at Vassar, too. "You don't need those girls, they're snobs."

Of course, Suzy was right. But still, Lise was hurt. Then puzzled by the sudden appearance of new girls—girls who had mysteriously discovered her origins. Other refugees. Lise felt as conspicuous as Hester Prynne; she might just as well have had an *R* on her forehead.

And, much as she hated to admit it, she didn't like these new girls with their heavily accented voices, their need to share confidences, their attitude that America owed them something. She was glad when the year was over and she could go home for the summer. Next fall she was pleasant to her new "friends," but somewhat aloof.

Now, though, one of them, a brilliant girl with a pockmarked face and handsome features, would not get out of her room.

"I have to get going, Marcia, I've got to pack. I'm supposed to go to Columbia tomorrow for Winter Weekend." Lise stood up, so Marcia did, too. When they reached the door, Lise thought, Thank God, we've avoided whatever she came here to say. But Lise was wrong.

At that moment Marcia whipped around and, towering over Lise, said, "You're too proud. You think you're better than the rest of us, that you're not a refugee because your family came early, but what you don't understand is that the goyim don't like Jews who talk like you do, who think they're Yankees, who act like they own the earth."

Lise stared. Her parents never used the word *goyim* and had also forbidden her and Leo to use it. Then she said, "We don't use that word, we have gentile friends we're very close to. And you have no right to tell me how to act."

"You're just what I thought, a typical German Jew, a first-class snob."

"We're from Vienna." This was getting almost laughable, Lise thought.

"Vienna, Germany, it doesn't matter to anyone but you, and maybe your precious parents." Marcia's face was almost ugly with contempt. "Let me tell you something. Here you're one thing and one thing only. A refugee, apart from the goyim and even from the other Jews. You'd better get that through your thick head." Then she was gone. Blessedly gone.

Lise wished she could talk to her father. Maybe he would have the right words to assuage anger like Marcia's. But it was too late to call. Even too late to mull. She fell into bed; the packing for Columbia would have to wait until tomorrow morning.

The winter this year had been freezing, colder than predicted, colder than anyone could remember. Trains were late, buses skidded into embankments, houses and schools flooded because of pipes that had burst. The only advantage in all the cold was a frozen river. On her way to Manhattan Saturday morning, Lise was cheered by the sight of the brightly clothed skaters swirling their intricate patterns on the resplendent, milky ice.

She had never said yes to a blind date before. But Suzy had been insistent. This young man was someone in Jake Huber's fraternity, and he was shy, but very nice. When Lise alighted from the train at Grand Central, he was there to meet her, and he had a pleasant, open face.

But with each passing hour Lise knew that this wasn't working out, and by late Saturday afternoon she had decided to plead sick. Before dinner she told him she didn't feel well and thought she'd better get back to Vassar. His relief was so transparent she couldn't even feel angry. And at least he had the sense not to insist when she said she would get herself back to the station. After he put her into a cab and solemnly paid the driver, he waved goodbye. Lise was so tired she dozed all the way downtown.

When she got to the warm, bustling station, though, she began to wake up. On the big board she saw that she had almost an hour before her train to Croton, where she would change for the train to Poughkeepsie. Quickly, she headed for the Oyster Bar. It was one of her father's favorite places; he said the Guastavino tile ceiling reminded him of a restaurant where he and Professor Wahrhaftig used to eat in Vienna. Lise loved it too: the steaming tiles, the informal atmosphere, the smell of the fish. As she stepped inside, unconsciously looking for her parents, her glance skimmed the back of various heads. For a moment her heart quickened. One man was surely Papa, but when he turned around he was much older than her father.

Should she go home? How pleased they would be to see her. But then she imagined her mother questioning her about her blind date. Mama worried continually that Lise was a bookworm and not having enough fun. Lise knew there was no way she could convince Mama she had done the right thing by leaving Columbia tonight. Still, it was tempting. She could see herself sitting with them in front of a blazing fire with one of Mama's old shawls around her shoulders, telling them about her date, and then about Marcia. Maybe now, once and for all, they could get this business about being refugees straight.

But no. As she sat there, letting the hot clam chowder almost burn her throat, Lise knew it would be better to figure this out on her own and get back to work on that *Wuthering Heights* paper. Go back to Poughkeepsie, the "safe harbor," she decided with a smile.

As soon as they pulled out of Grand Central she fell asleep, a small, squinched-up figure who looked no bigger than a child, for she had hardly grown in the ten years they had been in America. Five measly inches. And such tall parents and brother. She couldn't understand it and sometimes wondered if she might have been able to manage everything better if she had been taller.

But as soon as the train approached Honeywell, Lise's eyelids fluttered open, like a reflex. She could see the steeple of the Catholic church and the tops of the turrets of their house. As always in winter, the turrets were dark, but when the train lurched to a stop, Lise saw that the dining room was ablaze with light. How easy would be for her to dash from the train up the hill and burst in on them. How she would love to see the cake and fruit set out on the white linen cloth, and the silver coffeepot, still warm to the touch, glowing near Mama's elbow. Or the radiant faces of her parents' friends as they stirred their coffee and tried to finish one of Mama's rich desserts. Oh, why not go? Lise began to gather her belongings. A wild recklessness trilled through her. Of course she would go!

Yet by the time she had hurried down the aisle, the whistle was blowing and the train groaning to a start as it pulled out of the Honeywell station. Oh, well, perhaps it's for the best. I really ought to get that paper done, Lise thought, as she burrowed back into her seat.

The next day the dormitory was quieter than usual, even for a Sunday. Almost everyone had gone to a winter weekend somewhere. After working on her paper for several hours, Lise decided to get some air. She walked briskly across the campus and down toward the frozen river. Close up, the ice wasn't as glassy as it looked from the train, and way out Lise saw ice floes, stiff as statues, locked together in the dense, cold air. Nearer to her were skaters who stopped to warm their numb fingers at the bonfires on the edge of the ice. Most of them were children; their ruddy, expectant faces showed not a care in the world except whether they could skate backward or sustain a figure eight. The sight of them made her more homesick than she had been for the last two and a half years.

Standing there, watching the patterns of color on the ice, Lise saw not the sturdy children but her parents: her willowy, handsome parents dressed somewhat formally in a suit and skirt and jacket and layers and layers of thin wool clothing underneath, her father clasping her mother's waist as they pushed off on their cracked leather skates as easily as a pair of fairyland dancers.

"It's the closest thing to having wings," Mama always insisted. And now, in Lise's vision, they were flying together over the ice, never, not once, hesitating on the bumpy, pitted surface of the frozen Hudson—merely gliding and swirling through the bluish, dreamlike cold.

Slowly Lise walked back to the dorm; it was after two, and she was hungry and pressed because the paper wasn't coming as easily as she had expected. She also found herself wondering what they were doing now at Columbia and, for a moment, almost regretted her decision to come back early to this lonely campus. She was so engrossed that when she got back to the dorm she didn't hear the desk girl saying something to her. Only after the girl was actually running after her, with a message dangling from her hand, did Lise realize she was telling her, "Lise, your mom called, she wants you to call back."

Why would Mama be calling so early? How odd. She knew Lise was supposed to be at Columbia. Yet as soon as she heard her mother's voice, Lise's heart plummeted down through her body. And when Mama began to shriek into the telephone, "Arthur's gone! Arthur's gone!" it took Lise no more than a second to realize that *gone* was a euphemism for *dead*.

Two parallel rays of light piercing the darkness, each intent on its own way, unable to intersect. That is what the night became in Lise's mind. The train routinely speeding toward Poughkeepsie in the moonlit dark and the warm glow in her parents' home shining steadily until they said goodnight to their guests, tidied up the kitchen, and went through the house shutting out lights. Then bed, and in the morning an emergency patient or two, their Sunday walk down to the river where there were some skaters out already (prompting them to say that perhaps they would return later with their skates) and then past the stationer's where the Sunday *Times* and *Herald Tribune* awaited them as they had every week for the past ten years.

At home Arthur Hurwitz stirred the coals in the fireplace and added a log, and before Simone left to prepare lunch, a fire was burning brightly. While she waited for the leftovers to warm, Simone stared out the window at the purple finches scrabbling for food at the feeder. Vaguely, somewhere in the distance, she heard a peculiar sound, like water gurgling down a pipe. Irritated, she wondered how on earth they would find a plumber on Sunday. But when she inspected the sink in the kitchen and the one in the nearby bathroom, they were fine. And then it dawned on her, and when she rushed into the living room and saw her husband sitting so stiffly with the newspaper hanging slack from his hand, she knew he was dead.

Simone stood there, a striking figure in her mid-forties with still-dark chestnut hair parted in the middle and fastened behind her ears with glittering mother-of-pearl combs. She stood there and stared at Arthur, unable to touch him, thinking not about him or herself, but about her sisters. Since the *Anschluss,* she had spent three years getting used to the terrible fact that her sisters and their families were either imprisoned or dead. Letters no longer arrived and her letters simply disappeared, so she lived with continual silence. Silence so palpable she could taste it. Silence so omnipresent that it seemed to settle like a slowly festering sore onto her heart—a dullish bruise that was always there and hurt even when it was only slightly grazed. Yet now, out of the depths of that silence came her sisters' voices and their bold, hurtful questions when she told them she was going to marry Arthur Hurwitz.

Terrible questions, carefully buried for more than twenty-five years, began to ring in Simone's head that Sunday afternoon. Ringing and ringing so that she seemed crazed, and when she finally heard Lise's startled, "Hello?" she screamed into the telephone, "Arthur's gone! Arthur's gone!" as if her words had to carry across the entire span of the Atlantic Ocean, and then some. As if her words could break her sisters' frightening silence and answer those cruel, nagging questions.

When Lise arrived home later that day, she went to her father's notebooks: *Europe* and *The Hudson.* Each evening, no matter how late, Papa wrote in them. When Lise once asked him why, he confessed, a little embarrassed, that although his spoken and reading English were fine, he was ashamed of his written English. These notebooks forced him to practice it.

Vainly Lise searched for some clue that he might have known his heart was bad. But there was nothing in those meticulous notebooks that recorded the plight of Europe or gathered facts about the river and its history. Not a word.

The next day Lise heard her boots crunch across the icy path to his grave. The entire town of Honeywell had gathered for the funeral in the synagogue, but here in the cemetery were only the family and their close friends. While the rabbi intoned the prayers, the air was briefly fogged with the pluming breaths of the men who struggled to lower the glossy coffin into the ground. Lise felt sorrier for those men than she did for her father, for Papa wasn't really in that long box. This was just a play, a rehearsal for what might happen years and years from now—after she and Leo had married, after he had seen his grandchildren, after his hair and beard had turned a bright white that would make it easier to find him in a crowd.

"Come, Liselotte," her mother motioned her to take the shovel. Lise pushed a lump of frozen earth onto the coffin and tried not to hear the horrible thudding sound. Then some more people came forward, and again those thuds echoed into the cold, and just as Lise was convinced she would scream, Mama screamed: a shrill cry that lacerated the air as sharply as the shriek of a buzzard. Then it was over, and they stood back, letting the gravediggers tamp down the earth so the grave would be exactly level with the ones next to it.

Even after all that, she didn't believe it. She could see Papa waiting for them in the wing chair, marking what he was reading with his thick red pencil, and looking up when she entered the room, then removing his glasses and smiling at her as if he hadn't seen her for ages. He was always so glad to see her.

But the wing chair was empty.

Lise couldn't understand how so much food and so many people had found their way into the house, and she listened and watched while the others talked and ate, but she couldn't swallow. So she slipped away and went to her turret, her summer bedroom, where it was almost as cold as outside. Dragging an eiderdown from the closet, she wrapped herself in it and sat staring out the window. After a while, voices called to her, but she didn't answer or move. Her eyes were fixed on the intricate pattern of frost that had inched its way around the window. Then she looked through the shrunken pane of glass. Chunks of ice in the river were breaking up, and as they floated slowly downstream Lise thought of them as coagulated sins—lies, murders, treacheries, the *Wuthering Heights* paper she knew she would never write—bumping and banging their way through the gray-blue water that was several tones darker than the pewter sky.

For one thing she was thankful. At least the sun had had the grace to stay behind the clouds today. If it had been there in the cemetery, shaking its light around them, that would have been more than she could stand.

Then, out of nowhere, Lise felt someone grabbing her shoulders and she looked up into Leo's angry eyes. He was shouting, "Lise, for Christ's sake, why the hell didn't you answer? Mama's going crazy!"

Lise didn't know. She didn't know anything.

A Summer Dusk, 1944

For the life of her, she could never call him Emanuel to his face. Behind his back, sometimes, although she still preferred "Mr. Gray," but to his face, never. So she simply avoided addressing him directly, which made Lise feel like a child and annoyed her mother.

Tonight, though, she would try. For they had come on this first summer evening to celebrate D-Day at the Patroon Restaurant in Tarrytown. Surrounded by all the Hudson River lore her father loved, Lise was determined to make it a pleasant evening. It was three and a half years since Papa's death. At first Lise felt like a hibernating animal, seeking sleep whenever she could, but after a while she had been better able to function. Within a few months of graduating from Vassar, she had gotten a job doing plant research and Mama had married a childless widower from Boston who was doing everything he could to make Lise like him.

His solicitude was a burden. She often wished Leo were still at home so they could share it. But Leo was in the Army, in the office of a Japanese internment camp in

California because his heart murmur prevented him from going on active duty. And even if he weren't in the Army, Leo wouldn't be here. His heart was in the Midwest—he was engaged to a girl from Ann Arbor, a beautiful, self-confident girl named Norma, and after the war ended they planned to get married and live in Detroit or Chicago, where Leo would set up his law practice. If there were no war, Lise would still be dealing with Emanuel Gray by herself.

She spent hours, sometimes days, it seemed, wondering what it would be like if her mother hadn't remarried. She remembered those first two winters before she graduated, when she would come down almost every weekend from Poughkeepsie and help Mama with the house and all the paraphernalia of bills and insurance and selling Papa's practice.

They had done it, just the two of them, and Mama had been able to keep the house because they had found a young doctor named Harrison Gould to take over the practice. He had a house of his own, on a hill in Honeywell several blocks away. "My wife prefers not to live next to the office," he told Mama when she interviewed him.

Little by little, they had settled into a quieter life, a lonelier life, but Mama still had her friends and the activities at the synagogue. There was also enough money to buy good food and fine fabrics for Mama's sewing projects and bulbs and plants and peat moss for the still-magnificent garden, which announced each spring with a mass of yellow and white daffodils, the mottled creams and reds of the Kaufmanniana tulips, the sudden tight buds of the red emperors and the long-ago-pillaged hearts-ease.

There were even trips to New York—to the museums and the opera and theater—and if her mother moved more tentatively in public places than she had when Papa was alive, she was still a remarkably young and vibrant-looking woman around fifty. Papa would be proud to see how well Mama managed. Yes, he would be proud of them both, Lise decided.

Then her mother had gone to Boston for a much-needed change to spend a few weeks with Sally. And there was Emanuel Gray. He came into Lise's life with the suddenness of lightning, and she was still bewildered by his and her mother's remarriage. It had never occurred to her that her mother would marry again. Their life seemed so peaceful, so self-contained. And yet, when she thought about it rationally, Lise realized it was perfectly logical. Her mother was still young, still pretty; she shouldn't have to look forward to being alone for the rest of her life.

"She didn't want you to feel you had to stay home and take care of her forever," Cousin Sally said sensibly.

"And it does make her life more comfortable. Now she can keep the house and not worry about every small repair," Anna and Charlotte, the spinster sisters from Philadelphia added.

Even Mama offered Lise some comfort. "Second marriages aren't like first ones," she said shyly, one evening when they were sitting by the fire and Emanuel was away on a business trip. Mama took off her glasses and stared into the flames. Her dark eyes were velvet. "I knew I would never find anyone even remotely like your father. It would be impossible. But Emanuel is kind and we like to do the same things. No, darling, second marriages aren't like first ones. They can't be." Then she turned to Lise and said, in a tremulous voice, "One becomes so much more sensible as one gets older. I feel like my sisters these days. And now I understand why they were so upset when I brought

Arthur—Papa—home. But aren't we lucky that I was young and rash once?"

Her mother had no regrets. And, it seemed, not even any anger. What had happened had happened. Her beloved sisters were lost forever, and her adored husband was dead. Life went on. There was no choice. Lise envied her.

After the wedding, Emanuel seemed bent on repairing everything that was old or shabby in the Honeywell house. The first winter, it was insulated and the turrets winterized; the second year the kitchen was modernized. Although materials were terribly scarce, Emanuel seemed to have contacts all over the building industry (he had made his money in real estate), and night after night, he would sit in Papa's chair reading the *Wall Street Journal* and his countless business sheets and magazines. And scheme. Lise hated watching his eyes glow shrewdly with all his schemes. When people asked him what he did, he was blatantly honest: "I make deals," he would answer smugly. She sometimes wondered how she could continue to stay under the same roof with him.

But she had no place to go. Besides, the turret, now winterized, was like a separate apartment. "And I don't want you living in some fleabag in Manhattan, with all those wild sailors and soldiers on leave," Mama would say whenever she tried to bring it up. So Lise stayed and was polite, but there was always a strain between her and Emanuel in the elegant home where Lise had mistakenly assumed she would always feel utterly comfortable.

Tonight would be better, though, Lise had promised herself, and while they waited to get seated and her mother and Emanuel looked at some of the old prints, Lise stared out at the river. In the lingering dusk it reminded her of a long, lithe animal stretching, a sleepy lion or tiger flexing its muscles under a smooth tawny skin, not quite able to find a place for itself. Only later, after the sun had set, would it become calm, like a restless sleeper who is finally mollified by the right blanket.

Lise wished Papa were here. Every day of her life she still wished Papa were here. When will this awful angry grief begin to dissipate? she sometimes wondered.

The hostess appeared. Their table was ready. People smiled as they wove their way through the gay, busy dining room. Some of them she knew by name, some by sight, for her father had become a legend since his death. She was glad Mama was wearing the new navy silk dress she made last February and that she was in her new dress, too—her first store-bought dress that she purchased with her own money last month. A pale, pinkish linen dress that brought out the reddish glow of her hair and that, even Mama had to admit, was made very well.

As she sipped the icy Dubonnet, Lise began to relax and told Emanuel and her mother about the Dutch landowners along the Hudson—the Philipses and Van Cortlandts and Van Rensselaers—who had really been vulgar renegades. She took delicious pleasure in saying, "They cared only about money and exploited the local farmers. The whole area became a huge feudal estate."

Emanuel smiled and nodded at her. That was a surprise. Usually he was bored by what he called these "tedious historical details." Yet this evening he cocked his head toward her and was actually listening. So Lise went on; something commanded her to tell these stories her father told her. "There was one farmer, though, who revolted; his name was William Prendergast and he organized a group of farmers up in Hudson, New York, about twenty years before the revolution. It was a success and reforms were made, but then Prendergast and his large family were forced to leave and they made their way along the southern tier of the state, finally settling in Jamestown, which was named after Prendergast's son, James."

Emanuel continued to smile and soon their meal arrived. The conversation was benign, mostly about the war, but tonight Lise was determined not to react when Emanuel talked about the war as if it were his own convenient means of making more money. Never had she known anyone who loved money as much as Emanuel. But she controlled herself. For the war was almost over, it now seemed, and when that happened she wouldn't have to listen to this drivel.

Besides, the food was wonderful. As good as she remembered. Lise enjoyed each bite of her duck. But while they were waiting for dessert, a chilly wind seemed to sweep across the table. Mama pulled her paisley shawl more tightly around her shoulders; she and Lise watched Emanuel fill his pipe. Suddenly the silence seemed awkward, heavy.

Emanuel began to puff, then said, in a stiff voice that reminded Lise of brittle leaves crackling underfoot, "You know, Lise, you're grown now, and your mother isn't getting any younger."

Lise stared. Why this non sequitur? They had been talking about the Botanical Garden show a minute ago.

"And the winters in Honeywell are hard. Why, sometimes it seems as if there's only winter and summer, with hardly any spring or fall."

Lise looked at Mama, expecting to see an amused glance, but instead her mother was rummaging through her handbag.

"Isn't that a little extreme?" Lise asked Emanuel. "Besides, Mama always manages to find some spring and fall. She couldn't have such a wonderful garden if she didn't." What a ridiculous conversation this is, she thought.

"You're right, Lise, I am exaggerating, and there are four seasons," he conceded, "but you know, the house is really too big for the three of us. Much too big. And one of these days you'll be telling us that you've met someone and are going to get married, won't you?" Then he smiled what Lise always thought of as a sleazy smile, the same kind of smile he had when he announced he had made "a killing."

She sat straighter. There was nothing ridiculous about what he was saying now. She had better pay attention. She began to worry her napkin until she almost tore it to shreds, then she heard Emanuel say, "You know it would really be better for your mother if we were to sell the house. This is the right time; well-built houses are as scarce as hen's teeth, and you could make a good profit. You and Leo. The money's for you. Your mother and I don't want it. I have enough for both of us."

Finally Lise's eyes met her mother's: the same mother who used to kiss her so hard after they hadn't seen each other that Lise could feel their cheekbones scraping against each other's, the same mother who wanted only to be able to keep the house so Leo and Lise could bring their children to visit her in it, the same mother who seemed compelled never to leave this river that had meant so much to her first husband. But now all that had changed. Mama gave Lise an almost imperceptible shrug, but a sign to Lise of her defeat.

"You know, Lise, it would really be better for you to be in the city. You wouldn't have to commute, and you would see more young people and be able to go to concerts and plays much more easily." His raspy voice had gotten more confident. "And of course the piano is yours, we'll have it moved to wherever you live, and whatever else you want, too. After all, this war isn't going to last forever, and you don't want to be stuck in this small town all your life. In this burg?"

His voice dwindled, and finally Lise looked at her mother's brimming eyes and understood. But then, as if in slow motion, mother and daughter rose and walked stiffly toward the ladies' room. For a second, Lise thought, perhaps Mama has changed her mind, perhaps she will keep the house and divorce Emanuel and everything will be peaceful and calm again. But no. Her mother's face had that grayish cast it had for months after Papa died and her eyes were pleading with Lise to understand, not to make a fuss. They could be back in Pertisau. But, of course, they were not. They were here in America, and from the window Lise could see the Hudson and Mama's eyes were helpless, caught in a web of their own making. There were no choices anymore—because Papa was dead.

So Lise realized what she must do. She said the only thing she could say, "It's all right, Mama, I understand, and you know, Mr. Gray is right. The house is simply too big. It always was."

But then her mother folded Lise into her arms and together they clung to each other and cried. Women who were washing their hands looked strangely at them until Mama said, almost laughing through her tears, "We're perfectly fine, aren't we, Liselotte?" And after they had wiped their faces and were repairing their makeup, Mama turned to Lise and said, in a voice that Lise would hear forever in her dreams, in a voice too gay to be trusted, "Oh, Liselotte, that dress is absolutely perfect on you. The most wonderful color. Never in my wildest dreams did I think you would ever be able to wear that shade of pink!"

Diny, 1980

My mother's face bloomed with light, with that peculiar iridescence of skin that all great beauties have. When I was growing up, I would stare at her radiant features in wonder; and when I was older, after she had died, I realized that it was as if a strong Mediterranean light had descended from the sky and glanced off the tops of the trees and roofs and then landed in its full glory on her face.

Was it because of the odd translucence of her skin or her glowing reddish hair that never browned with age, even after a streak of white suddenly and dramatically appeared on one side of her head? Or was it because of the extraordinary mobility of her features, or her vibrant grayish eyes that seemed to register every nuance of emotion she experienced?

I don't know, but whenever I imagine my parents I see my mother's special glow reflecting from her face to his, enclosing them both in a circle of light as beautiful, as comforting as the pool of lamplight when you sit, reading, in a darkening room. I see it in my mind as I saw it in their life: when they bent toward each other while they talked, when he stood near the piano watching her play, if he stretched his long frame on the sofa with his head on her lap, or, less frequently, when her head was in his lap. You could see it when they were yards apart in a theater lobby, or in a restaurant, or visiting school on parents' night.

Did my mother's face have that remarkable light before she met my father? Hard to know. You can't really see it in photographs, although my Grandma Simone has always said Lise had the most alive face of anyone she ever saw. Yet when I think of my mother closing the house in Honeywell in December 1944, there is no light on her face. Instead, it seems enclosed in a gray sadness; there is a glazed dullness in her eyes, as if she can't quite believe this is happening.

I know that that day was cold and dreary. As my mother walked through the large rooms of the house, she could still see the mauve-colored Palisades, those unusual vertical rocks that the Indians named "Weehawken" because they looked like rows of trees. But after about an hour or so, the Palisades disappeared from sight. A thick fog was stretching itself up from the river, and little by little, most of Honeywell became hidden. As my mother went through the house, now huge in its yawning emptiness, she was gripped by sudden panic, for she no longer had the familiar landmarks of the last thirteen years around her. She and the empty house now existed in a vacuum, and soon even the carefully pruned and mulched roses of her mother's garden were covered by fog.

Her mother had sold the house for what Emanuel Gray called "a song" to the Gould family, even though the broker said it was a fair price. And now Grandma Simone and Emanuel were in Florida looking for an apartment in

Palm Beach, and my mother was on her way to Boston. She had decided that she would stay with Cousin Sally for a while and try to find a job there, at least until the war was over. The piano was to stay in the house with the Goulds until she wanted it.

Although my mother was supposed to be checking the doors and windows of the Honeywell house, she hurried through it in a trance; she could think only about her father. She kept seeing his frown of disapproval. By selling the house they had broken his trust, he seemed to be saying to her. Yet how could she begin to explain when she didn't quite understand how this had happened?

Besides, how can you explain anything to a dead man?

By the time I saw the Honeywell house, the house my mother referred to as the Gould house and the rest of the people in town called the Hurwitz house, it was badly in need of a paint job, and the garden had deteriorated into a tangle of weeds. Grass refused to take hold, perhaps because it had once been so completely usurped by the healthy phlox and delphinium and iris and lilies and asters and yarrow and thistle that my grandmother planted and nurtured. The majestic lines of the house were still obvious, though, and whenever my mother passed it, her face would change: that radiant light would dim slightly, and her skin would take on a peculiar cast that was reminiscent of something I had seen when I was very small. It was what I called "the gray sadness."

The first time I saw it my mother had come home after what seemed a very long absence. She was standing on a stool in her bedroom, reaching onto the upper shelf of the closet and then pulling out what appeared to be a huge pillow to my young eyes, but which I know now was an eiderdown. A rose-colored quilt that I had never seen before, but whose very touch seemed to calm her, give her comfort. I slept under its massive bulk for a few months, and then it disappeared when she disappeared. And when she returned again, there was no mention of the eiderdown, and the gray sadness in her face was gone.

The second time I saw that awful sadness was the day she died. But that will come later.

Most of the time, though, my mother's face had its usual vivid glow. When she was alone, it gave her the look of having a great secret, and when my parents were together it became part of something shared—that mysterious something that never failed to startle me even though I saw it almost every day of my life.

Murray, 1945

1

When Lise walked through the main door of the laboratory that was known as Branson's Lab, she was reminded of those feelings she had had on hurrying through the gothic Taylor Gate at Vassar each fall: of that sharp quiver of excitement when she ran up the stairs to the drab, foul-smelling labs. For she knew it was here, in these practical cheerless spaces, that she would spend her happiest hours, while the muscles in her neck tightened to a rigid cord and she peered down the thin shaft of the microscope.

Yet she was a very different person from the girl who had gone to Vassar. Her father was dead, and the man her mother had thought would help them keep the house had somehow engineered its sale. So now Lise was in Boston with Sally—at least until the war was over and apartments in New York less scarce.

After the new year Sally had told her that she had arranged for an interview with a brilliant biologist she knew, Murray Branson.

"You're early," the receptionist greeted her.

"I know. I just moved here and wasn't sure how long it would take to get here." Since when did you have to apologize for being early? Lise wondered.

"Have a seat," the girl said. Her voice was weary. Soon Lise saw why. She was both receptionist and lab technician, shuttling between the tiny waiting room and the unknown space behind the frosted glass door marked *Only Lab Personnel Admitted.* The only other person Lise saw in the hour and a half that passed while she sat there reading *Sense and Sensibility,* which Sally had thrust into her hand when she left the house, was a janitor who smiled when he looked at her.

Oh, why was she here? Murray Branson was a well-known researcher; when she had called her biology teacher at Vassar, the woman had known who Branson was. All Lise had to offer him was two years' experience in a plant research lab and a few months as a secretary for a virus lab. Besides, she had found two of his papers, and they were learned and literate. He probably had a slew of people working here and didn't need anyone young and inexperienced. He was simply humoring Sally by seeing her, and now it looked as if he had forgotten. He said to come at ten-thirty, and it was almost twelve. Maybe she'd better slip out and go home. That harried girl would never remember. And next time she would get her own interview. She stood up.

But the receptionist was back. Don't be foolish, Lise said to herself. Besides, she couldn't embarass Sally. "I beg your pardon," she said as she approached the desk, "but I've been waiting for Dr. Branson for almost two hours." Just as the girl shifted her eyes nervously, the frosted door opened, and a tall man in a plaid flannel shirt and corduroy pants and saddle shoes said, "Miss Hurwitz?"

Another delay! Lise's heart dropped. She was getting nauseated with nerves and hunger, but she said nothing and followed him into an office scarcely bigger than a closet.

When he turned and raised his dark slashes of eyebrows, she said sharply, "I've been here since ten-fifteen."

"I know. It's ridiculous, sometimes this whole place is ridiculous. We were working on some timed cultures and when the appointment was made we didn't know we would be up all night with them. I went home for some shut-eye and overslept." His voice was low, so nasal it sounded as if he were wearing a clothespin on his nose. Lise wanted to laugh for the first time in months. But she didn't, and now his deep, almost black eyes were taking in her face. His stare became so intense that Lise was embarrassed; all she needed now was for one of Branson's assistants to make a pass.

Suddenly he came around to the front of his desk and sat down on its corner. For such a tall person, he was oddly graceful. She could imagine him playing tennis, or golf, then wondered what malady might have kept this handsome, apparently healthy young assistant out of the Army.

"So where is this famous Dr. Branson who keeps people waiting as if they had nothing else in the world to do?" she finally demanded. She didn't want any more of this self-confident assistant. Her chin jutted forward, as it always did when she was getting angry.

"Right here," the young man said, then raised those dark slashes again, his eyes shimmering with amusement. "I'm Murray Branson. I thought you knew."

2

After the interview Lise didn't see much of Murray Branson. He didn't pay much attention to his lab assistants, and although he wandered through Lise's part of the lab every few days and she occasionally felt his black eyes on her, she never gave it much thought. Those fierce dark eyes bore holes wherever they looked; they were simply part of his personality.

One hot, humid night in June, Lise found herself the last one in the lab. She was going over some statistical material, and she hadn't realized how late it was. When she looked at her watch, she saw it was after seven; and when she craned her neck to check the thermometer outside, she saw that it was ninety-seven degrees. If she were back in Honeywell, she would surely find a way to swim in the river tonight. When she closed her eyes, she could feel its coolness, like a refreshing breeze against her cheek. Oh, how she longed to be back there, near that changeable, whispering stretch of water!

But as soon as she thought of the river, Lise's thoughts turned to her mother. She owed Mama a letter. What was there to write? Mama wanted to hear about dates and young men, but there were no young men. Or hardly any. And if she tried to write about her work, she would receive querulous, scolding letters that couldn't have been written by the mother she knew. Yes, Mama had changed; she was unhappy in Florida, she missed her garden, the seasons, her beautiful home, Honeywell. And her children, too. So, because she couldn't admit any of that, she wrote awful letters—critical, carping letters—behind which she could hide her aching heart.

"Why you insist on hiding your beautiful face behind

a microscope, test tubes, and those dangerous Bunsen burners, I will never understand. And as for your Dr. Branson, if he's so important and so intelligent, why did he interview you in clothes that sound like the ones Leo wore in high school?" her mother had written recently. When she received letters like that, Lise longed for her father's reasonable voice quieting her mother, calming her, explaining, "The best minds go into research, they always have, even when I was young. That's where the excitement is."

But Papa was dead, and her mother had been transformed by the dull weather in Florida. Just thinking about it depressed her. Lise folded her hands on the desk in front of her and put her head down. Perhaps if she could take a little catnap, she wouldn't feel so awful.

She didn't know quite how, but soon she sensed another presence in the lab, and when she raised her head she thought: Well, Mama would approve of Murray Branson's clothes today. For, on this hottest evening of the year, he was wearing a long-sleeved shirt and tie, gray worsted slacks, and black oxfords. While she was a rumpled mess. Her navy silk shirt that had been so smart at eight A.M. was now stuck to her back, wrinkled under the arms and across the front, and her white skirt, of that new miracle fabric rayon, was turned at the waist. God knows what my face must look like, Lise thought, all too aware of her body because her deodorant no longer had much effect on the sweat that was dripping along the insides of her arms and around her waist and between her breasts.

But when she observed Branson more closely, she saw that he looked as tired and hot as she felt. His hair was tangled with all the times his fingers had gone through it—no one could miss that nervous habit of his—and as he stood there, he was loosening his tie and rolling up his sleeves.

"Lise, can you stay?" He stepped toward her. How bloodshot his eyes were! He had probably been working around the clock for days and must have had a meeting with some big-wigs this afternoon. Now she vaguely remembered hearing about it, and that would surely explain his clothes.

How could she refuse? She had nothing to do. Hesitating for a moment, she bent her head to mark her place on the data she was reading, and when she looked up Murray Branson's eyes were soft, almost gentle. But only because she was another pair of hands. People swore he didn't know if his lab assistants were men or women—he simply saw them as two eyes, two arms, and ten fingers. Lise thought that was a little extreme; no man was that oblivious, especially if he was under thirty. Moreover, she had once seen Branson in a bar on the waterfront with a woman, a tarty-looking woman, she remembered. So he couldn't be that extreme.

Of course, she would stay. He was exhausted. Besides, they got overtime.

"Sure," she said, as casually as she could, and came around to the front of her desk and leaned against it. She didn't want him to feel beholden to her; it was merely chance that she was the only one left in the lab and he was asking a favor of her. Yet as she stood there, listening to him explain some of the fine points of his experiment, Lise could feel herself staring at the hairs on his forearms—dark brown, almost chestnut hairs, lighter than the very dark hair on his head—and she felt herself wanting to reach out and touch those hairs, she wanted to run her fingers lightly along them so she could feel the tendons that were visible under his too-white skin, the giveaway that he worked too hard. Much too hard. When did he relax, or go out? And only at night for what her brother Leo always called so coarsely "a quick lay"? Oh, there were so many things she would have liked to know about him!

But of course Lise didn't touch him. How can you touch someone you barely know? So, instead of moving toward him when he started to show her a scrap of paper, she stepped back, along the side of her desk. Then he opened the folder he had put down and when he found what he wanted, he straightened and began to move toward her again. Almost to prove to herself that she didn't feel anything for this man who had almost totally ignored her since that strange interview five months ago, Lise stepped forward, too, and in that simultaneous motion Murray Branson's fingers accidentally grazed her breast. Lise could feel her nipple harden, and she thanked God she was wearing navy.

Yet when their eyes met, she knew that he had felt it, too, and that he wasn't staring into undifferentiated space at all, but was gazing at her in an entirely new way. She knew it was no coincidence that they were both in the lab this late on such a boiling hot day, and that he had not been ignoring her at all, but fighting something in himself that he could no longer deny.

3

Murray Branson had thought he would never marry. Even as a small boy growing up in the Sheepshead Bay section of Brooklyn, in a large, mostly contented family, with every material comfort he would ever need, Murray had always thought he would be alone. Love, companionship, marriage didn't seem to be part of his birthright. He didn't know exactly why, it wasn't something you discussed, and besides, the idea rested most of the time in his unconscious.

Perhaps he had it because he was so much more intellectual than his parents and brothers and sisters. And then, when he was discovered to be a math and science genius, his expectations seemed fulfilled. Quietly, Murray resigned himself to the life of a scientist. Alone.

He was the fourth in a family of five children. His two older sisters he barely knew. By the time he was ten, they had married two brothers from Chicago and moved there. His brother Harry was six years older than he, and his brother George fifteen years younger. But Murray was the star. While everyone else went to neighborhood schools, Murray was sent to the famous, competitive Stuyvesant High School, and then to Harvard College. From the time he was seventeen he lived in Boston. After he had published his doctoral thesis on the effect of viruses on genes, he joined the staff of one of the most famous laboratories in the country. It was run by Herman Davison, who was convinced he could discover the composition of genes.

Murray Branson worked harder than anyone in Davison's lab, so hard that he didn't even know the United States was at war until his brother Harry finally reached him at eleven o'clock at night on December 7, 1941. He was twenty-six years old, in good health, and about to be drafted. But Davison was a canny man; he wrote a proposal for his lab to study the genetic effects of poison gas and other weapons, and his best disciple was ordered, against his own wishes, to stay at the Boston lab. Within a year, though, Herman Davison was dead—of a massive heart attack—and until they could reorganize the lab, it was run by the gifted Murray Branson.

As head of the lab, Branson drove himself with an intensity seldom seen, even in that high-powered scientific community. He rarely had time for anything but work and went out only to official lab parties. Occasionally there were women, but never for very long. In his memory they became anonymous combinations of hair, eyes, mouths, breasts, legs, voices. It was the voices he remembered best. Somehow, he couldn't imagine spending the rest of his life with any of those voices.

Then, one day, when he was convinced that nothing, not even this endless experiment he was working on, would be of any use, this small, beautiful woman carrying a copy of *Sense and Sensibility* sat herself down in his office. Her gray eyes reminded him of lights you suddenly spy when you're driving at night in a fog, just at the point when you think you'll have to pull over. Beautiful gray lights shining out of a milky, heart-shaped face. And when she spoke, her lilting voice filled his tiny closet of an office.

He could listen to it forever, he thought.

4

Warm October light filled the sky. The war was over, and Lise and Murray were going to New York, where Murray had a job interview and where Lise would meet Murray's brothers, Harry and George, and Harry's wife, Rose. It was a perfect day, and as the old green Oldsmobile wound its way along the coast road from Boston to New York, Lise could sense that wonderful, drenching saltiness that blew in across the dunes and had already begun to seep into the closed-up houses along the shore.

"It reminds me of the Hudson in the spring," she told Murray. Then she spotted an elderly couple ambling across the sand. In their leisurely pace was a well-earned freedom from the calendar and work. Their white heads bent toward each other as they walked and talked. That was what she had dreamed of for her parents, and the sight of those innocent strangers, surrounded by a cluster of cawing gulls, sent a lump to Lise's throat. She was amazed, then ashamed that such a harmless sight could cause her such pain.

"That's what they deserved," she told Murray.

"Deserved? That's a strange word, Lise. What does it mean?"

"Papa had planned. And because he had planned he got us out of there. For that alone he deserved to grow old."

Murray smiled. "Having the foresight your father had, doesn't assure anyone of anything, darling. And being intelligent doesn't, either."

She shook her head. They had had this discussion before. But Murray didn't really understand. And she had finally decided that he couldn't understand. So she shook her head and nestled into the old, cracked, leather seat that had such a strange, yet pleasant smell, and dozed.

While Lise slept, Murray made his way to a beach in Connecticut he had known since he was in college. One of his roommates had had a summer place there. Slowly he eased the car to a stop, and soon the lack of motion woke Lise. When she opened her eyes she was dazzled by the blinding brightness: The world had been brushed with a lavish stroke of gold.

They got out of the car and made their way across the pebbly beach, two stick shadows lengthening as the day drew to a close. Near the water they sat down and took off their shoes. The water was so calm it barely rippled, and when it slid over their toes it was surprisingly warm. Far warmer than Lise expected.

Harry and Rose Branson's Long Island house sat on

a manicured swath of green, its outside lines softened by the right number of azaleas and rhododendrons and laurels, under which impatiens and begonia still bloomed. Exactly the sort of landscaping Lise's mother abhorred: forest plants jammed in front of a house with no wit or imagination. The inside was large, what Papa used to describe as "a house with a lot of rooms." Lise was shown through every last one, at Rose's elbow, while Rose told her all about her decorator. Yet there was not a cozy spot in the entire house. Still, she kept smiling, even when Rose stopped several times to exclaim, "What a little bit of a thing you are, Murray never mentioned how small you are."

Yet she could see how pleased Murray was to be here. He and Harry and George (who was still in high school and lived with Harry and Rose since Murray's mother had died) had hugged each other in greeting, and as she walked through the house with Rose, Lise could see the three of them in the garden talking and walking with their arms around each others' shoulders. So she smiled and nodded as often as she could.

But after Rose's grand tour, Lise could feel a headache coming on. When Rose suggested a cup of coffee, she begged off and said she'd like to lie down. It was only four-thirty, and dinner was at seven. She needed a little time to collect herself. Besides, she wanted to finish "The Beast in the Jungle." But when Rose showed her up to her room, Lise was too tired to read or even to turn down the bedspread. All she wanted to do was sleep.

When she stretched and turned she saw that it was almost six o'clock. Above the ticking of the clock she could hear voices, raised voices. Quietly, she tiptoed to the door of the bedroom and opened the door. It didn't make a sound on the thick, buttery carpet. She heard the word *accent* a few times, and then, "She has a very slight accent. But that's not what matters—why, she looks as if she'll blow over in a wind. And she doesn't seem to be in the least bit interested in domestic things. She was bored to tears when I showed her the house." Rose's voice carried up the stairs.

Then Lise could hear Murray's nasal voice. "She's not interested in domestic things. She's a biologist. She works every day, just like me. And she doesn't have an accent. But even if she did, who would care? Not me, for sure. And you're wrong, Rose. She's as strong as an ox, she works harder than almost anyone else in the lab, and she's highly intelligent—she's practically an authority on respiratory viruses!" He sounded so exasperated Lise had to smile.

"A lot of good that'll do her raising a family," Rose replied, then some clanking of dishes.

A few minutes later, Harry's voice, low, concerned, "Are you sure, Murray? This is a big step, marriage is no joke, you know . . ."

Lise closed the door. She felt like an animal up for auction. She slipped on her shoes and threw some cold water on her face and straightened her hair. If she appeared they would have to stop this nonsense. When she went into the hall, she heard, "I think she's wonderful." A new voice. A young voice. George. "Absolutely wonderful, and beautiful. Exactly the kind of woman I would like to marry."

How young, how naïve George sounded. His ingenuousness was such a contrast to Rose's sharp, pecking tone. Lise hurried down the stairs. When she entered the breakfast nook, Murray was concentrating on his drink as if he were an alcoholic, but Rose was perfectly poised. Her turquoise eyes met Lise's. "I'm so happy for you," she said, then straightened Lise's collar, which had become crushed while she napped. "And I hope you'll give yourself some time to find an apartment and get settled before you start working." Lise stared. She barely knew this woman.

She looked at Murray. He was staring out the window. From the set of his head she knew he was furious. And when his eyes met hers, she saw that he was ashamed at what she might have overheard. But he was too miserable to help her now. So Lise smiled again. She didn't know what else to do; she had never met people like Rose and Harry before. She was still smiling when Rose added, with a slight edge to her voice, "Oh, and the next time you nap, Lise, dear, please turn down the spread. They charge a small fortune to have those bedspreads cleaned."

Murray's interview was at two at Sloan-Kettering. An old professor of his had called, there was a job that would be a challenge. Murray welcomed the opportunity to leave the Boston lab, for Davison's shadow hung over all the work done there. It also seemed a perfect opportunity to get back to New York, where Lise wanted to live.

It went well, and he was offered the job. When he came out of the interview, Murray swooped Lise into his arms and together they glided across Sixty-eighth Street and past Hunter College. Rose was expecting them for dinner—one of her famous Friday night dinners—but they had no intention of going back there. No, they would call with some excuse, they had met friends and were staying in town for the evening or the professor insisted on having dinner with them—anything to avoid that stifling house— and they would drive to Long Island in the morning to collect their belongings before returning to Boston.

Like giddy teenagers, they stopped at Woolworth's; and in the soft tawny light that had spread through the city, Lise slipped the cheap, imitation-gold band onto her left ring finger. Dizzy with desire, they flew once again down the streets toward the Plaza Hotel. They had been lovers in Boston, but never before had they known such pleasure, such tenderness. Lise had not even dared to hope for anything like this; and all that afternoon and evening and night, walking with Murray, having a meal at Christ Cella, shopping for a nightgown, pajamas, toothbrushes, making love, Lise was filled with wonder that this was happening to her, to them. It seemed miraculous, as marvelous as the kaleidoscope of autumn colors on the trees the next morning. She was filled with awe and happiness as they made love one more time, and thoughts of the lab, of the war, of Honeywell, of her lonely piano, Emanuel Gray, Rose Branson, and even her father receded in her mind.

Summer, 1954

1

Lise Hurwitz and Murray Branson were married in Sally's house in Brookline on Christmas Day, 1945. They moved to Riverside Drive in New York at the beginning of 1946, and once again Lise and the Hudson River were daily companions. Although their apartment was much smaller and the spaces very different from the rambling Honeywell house she had loved, Lise felt that she had come home.

Murray went to work at Sloan-Kettering and Lise got a job in a virus lab run by a friend of Murray's, a man named Abe Goodside, at Mount Sinai. The Steinway grand was moved from the Goulds' house, and Lise finished furnishing the apartment—mostly with old pieces that had belonged to her parents and had been stored—about a month before their first child, Arthur Hurwitz Branson, was born in November 1946.

Weeks turned into months, then into years. Their lives were busy, filled with work and their child and each other. They saw the Bransons on holidays; Simone and Emanuel Gray sometimes came to New York and then there would be a Hurwitz family reunion; and once a year they met Leo and his wife, Norma, for Simone's birthday in Palm Beach. Suzy Huber married a man named Stanley Cahn, and they lived nearby, on Central Park West; Lise and Murray went to the theater and concerts and an occasional opera (Murray wasn't crazy about opera) with the Hubers and other friends—mostly colleagues they had met at work. Lise tried to play the piano a few times a week, she and Murray still spent long evenings reading and listening to music, and as she watched the seasons change she would sometimes wonder how time could flow by so quickly. It was like a ribbon so smooth she could never hope to grab it. Oh, she still missed her father, and there were days when a small incident or even a phrase could bring a pang to her chest, but she didn't dwell on those painful moments. She couldn't. There wasn't time.

She was even lucky with help. An elderly Englishwoman came for an interview when Arthur was almost two and Lise had decided to go back to work part time. She was perfect. Each morning Nanny Collins would arrive to take care of Arthur until Lise returned at three in the afternoon.

A second child, Diane, was born in the fall of 1951. Unlike her brother, who had his father's almost black hair and eyes, Diny inherited her mother's red hair and light eyes. When Arthur was almost eight, Lise and Murray decided to send him to overnight camp with Suzy and Stanley's children. Suzy and her brother, Jake, had gone there when they were children, and the camp was still run by the same family. "It's in the Adirondacks, old-fashioned, rustic, not too competitive. The cabins are nestled in woods filled with pine needles, and the lake is gorgeous," Suzy told them. Lise met the directors and saw pictures of the camp. It seemed a perfect place for a city kid to spend the summer.

Nanny Collins had warned her, but she hadn't listened. She had stubbornly insisted on going to Grand Central Station with both children by herself. Now, as Lise looked around the wild confusion of the main level, she knew that Nanny had been right. She should have left Diny home. But some strange compulsion had been working within her, and she had wanted to take Diny with her to see Arthur off to camp.

What looked like millions of children and their parents milled around the main waiting room of the station. Each camp was identified by a huge banner with its name and color. Her children tugged at her arms; from the feel of their hands in hers, she knew they were frightened: Diny of this enormous crowd and Arthur of the prospect of leaving her.

Why hadn't she let Nanny come with her? And why was Murray in Philadelphia at a meeting? And why was it so important to her that Diny see Arthur off to camp?

You have two hands, have two children, her father had sometimes told his young patients. But now two seemed one too many.

Finally she spotted Arthur's camp, and soon she saw Suzy and Stanley and their boys. But getting through the crowd was a job, and by the time they reached the place where Arthur's camp was gathering, Lise had barely time to greet the director and kiss Arthur goodbye. In what seemed like seconds, he was spirited behind that wide, copen-blue felt band that separated the campers from their waving families. The din was fierce, and Diny had begun to cry. Lise picked her up and they stood there together,

Diny crushed against the linen of her blouse. Lise felt her heart sink at the sight of Arthur's sad, brown, glossy eyes. Maybe he was too young to send away, she thought, as she and Diny watched the campers march bravely into the bowels of the station. But there was nothing she could do now.

Of course she was wrong. He wasn't even homesick. "He has made a remarkable adjustment," the head counselor wrote after the first two weeks. And at least he didn't have to cope with the soggy New York heat, Lise told herself again and again as she headed home each afternoon, missing him more than she could ever have imagined.

Visiting Day didn't come a moment too soon; they had a wonderful time. Arthur looked as if he had grown at least two inches. He was tanned, he liked the other boys, and the mountains, the swimming, and the canoeing. He had even hiked the trail to Lake Tear of the Clouds, where Lise and Murray and Suzy and Stanley were going after they left camp.

"You'll love it, Mom, it's the quietest place in the world, and the trail's not all that hard," he told them solemnly when she held him to her at the end of the long, delicious day. He smelled of campfire and marshmallows and the sweetness of eight-year-old sweat.

2

A tiny glimmering lake surrounded by stands and stands of the sweetest balsam imaginable. On the bank, a campsite with a smoldering fire and two old-fashioned green canvas tents. A small, very delicate-boned woman has lifted the flap of one tent and tiptoed to a tree to sit down. Her eyes

glow with surprise and pleasure. This small lake has shim-
mered like a gem in her memory: Lake Tear of the Clouds.
"The place where the river begins," her father called it.
Now ice skins skim along its surface and though they will
be gone soon, the water in Lake Tear is still the coldest
she has ever felt. Colder than the Hudson or the Aachen
See. So pure and cold no fish can live in it.

Lise sat there and let facts about Lake Tear crowd into
her mind: how Emmons and Hall had been hired in 1837
to trace the Hudson to its source, how they stopped before
they reached Lake Tear, venturing only as far as Feldspar
Brook. And how it was up to Verplanck Colvin to find
this "minute, unpretending tear of the clouds" in 1872.

It was easy to see how Emmons and Hall missed it.
She and Murray and Suzy and Stanley had passed Avalanche
Lake and Lake Colden at the northern end of the Opalescent
River and then went on to Calamity Brook, which was,
oddly, calm. When Stanley said, "We're approaching the
Opalescent," Lise envisioned another bubbling brook; in-
stead they found an angry river with fifty-foot waterfalls
and flumes eighty feet deep. Yet where the Opalescent and
Feldspar tributaries joined, the water was suddenly still,
and Emmons and Hall mistook it for the Hudson's source.
Only when you walked to the end of Feldspar Brook, as
Colvin did, could you see how it traveled through a steep
gorge and stopped here at Lake Tear.

Papa should have come and walked these trails. But
he had thought the terrain was wilder than it is. Now Lise
could see his benign expression as he rhapsodized about
his Hudson. Contented, she sat against the tree, feeling
its rough bark dig into her back, trying to ignore the
nausea that tugged at the pit of her empty stomach.

Hudson. Henry Hudson. In her imagination he had

always looked like Hans Brinker with the silver skates. His grandfather was a London alderman involved with the Muscovy Company, and Henry went to work for him, taking two voyages from Spitsbergen to Novaya Zemlya, which always sounded to Lise like something from *Alice in Wonderland*. On his third voyage, searching for the Northwest Passage, he landed in North America. He thought the river he had found went to Asia, but even if he had known about the Appalachian range and the Adirondacks, he would probably never have suspected that the river's source was this lonely, unassuming spot.

Now the sun was throwing a waxy gloss of light across the melting ice. Lise felt her eyes begin to tear. The tang of balsam filled her nostrils. Other campers stirred, snapping twigs broke the silence. That's what she should have been doing, but she didn't move. Lazily, she dozed. After a bit she shifted, and though her eyes were still closed, she sensed someone watching her. Expecting the curious glance of a stranger, Lise looked up; but it was Murray, his eyes blinking as he stepped from the dark drapery of their tent, his hair tousled, his clothes awry.

"I had this awful feeling you had disappeared, that I would never see you again, when I woke up. It must have been part of my dream, but now I can't remember what I dreamt," he told her, then pulled her head into the crook of his neck.

What an absurd idea, she thought, and her laughter rippled along the length of the clearing. She knew she was waking the others, but she couldn't stop—the laughter welled up from an inexhaustible source within her—and soon Murray was laughing, too, then kissing her, lifting her into his arms. As it skimmed the bed of pine needles, Lise's body was as fluid as water, and she felt dizzy. But this had happened before, lots of times before; it was simply how her body reacted to Murray, what those romantic novels called "weak in the knees," she supposed. She was sure it had no other significance, for how could she be pregnant and so happy all at once?

3

But she was deluded in that fragrant retreat. When they arrived home, the nagging nausea was with her morning, noon, and night. If she had been regular, she would have missed her second period by now. She knew she had to discuss it with Murray, yet each day she found herself hesitating. It seemed incredible that she was in this spot. She believed in abortion intellectually, yet going through one herself was something she had never imagined.

Still, there was no choice—neither she nor Murray had ever contemplated having a third child. They had a boy and a girl, their family was complete. And she knew exactly what she had to do. Only yesterday Suzy had given her a name. "He's a urologist, and he does it right there in his office. You rest for a while and you're home by dinnertime. I'll go with you, Lise," Suzy had said in the most matter-of-fact voice.

No big deal. So why was she making more of it than it was?

"Abortion?" Murray's eyes were startled.

"Yes, abortion," she said calmly, lacing her fingers on the table in front of her. "We didn't plan to have another child, we have a boy and a girl. In another three years, when Diny is in first grade, I can work full time. If we have this baby, I won't be able to do that for another six years," Lise replied. Her voice was low, hoarse. They were having coffee, Diny was asleep, the walls of their apartment were as thick as the pyramids, yet she needed to whisper. "When Abe Goodside told me I could take a few years before going back full time, I don't think he was counting on another six," she added. If there was one thing she and Murray agreed on, it was that she should work. In that, they were light years ahead of most people they knew.

But his frown was etching itself deeper on his face.

"Do you really want another child?" Lise's voice was rough.

"I'm not sure." He paused. "No, I wouldn't have ever said I wanted another child, but not wanting another child when you're talking abstractly about whether to have one is different from having an abortion after you're pregnant." He stopped and ran his hand through his hair—still thick black hair, Lise noted absently. "And you can work full time whenever you want, we can move to a bigger place and get a housekeeper."

"I don't want a housekeeper! You know how I feel about being home when a baby is small, at least most of the time. You used to feel that way, too!" she accused him.

Murray stared at her. "You're so sure of yourself, I envy you," he began. Then he stopped, but he didn't need to say it; she could see it and feel it—his fear, his uncertainty. How vulnerable he suddenly was. And when he finally said, awkwardly, "I know this may surprise you, Lise . . . even shock you, but I can't help feeling it's a life, our lives, or an extension of them . . ." He shrugged.

He wants this baby, Lise thought. She tried to make her voice calm, reasonable. "But can't you understand what will happen to my life if we have this baby?" she said.

"To my life, too, to all of us, to Arthur and Diny, as well," he replied. "Another baby will change everything, but maybe it will be for the better. Maybe we are exactly the sort of people who should have three children: healthy, able to support them, still young. I don't know, Lise, but I can't be so matter-of-fact about it. I keep thinking it was fated, and maybe we shouldn't play around with fate."

She stared at him. She couldn't believe that her husband, the well-known scientist who had said he never believed in anything but science, was talking about fate. She didn't know how to respond, so she looked down at her hands, which were no longer laced together in ladylike fashion, but were now fists fighting with each other in her lap. She tried to stop them, but she couldn't; those agitated fists had a life of their own. Like this baby.

But now Murray had moved closer to her and was reaching for those nervous hands. "You can't believe it—me talking about fate, Lise. I can hardly believe it, either, but all I can think is that it's a life, our life, not two sets of anonymous chromosomes. It's overwhelming, and when I think about destroying it, I'm uncomfortable. More than uncomfortable. Miserable. And scared," he added. Then he dropped her hands and stood up.

His tall body, usually so graceful and straight, now looked awkward, weary. And his eyes were suddenly glazed. What he looked like at that brief moment made a deeper impression on Lise than what he had said. Murray had raised questions she hadn't dared to ask herself. She had thought she was finished with pregnancy and infants, and she wanted to go back to work. But now she saw that it was far more complicated than she had realized.

Lise rose and began to clear the table. When they next looked at each other, Murray appeared more like himself; now such fierce love poured from his eyes that Lise thought he was going to remind her of that weekend the baby had been conceived, how lovely it had been. But no, she admitted to herself, *she* might try to do that to *him,* but he would never resort to such a cheap trick. No, he didn't want to persuade her of anything now; all he wanted was time.

"Let's think about this for a while, Lise. This isn't the sort of decision we can make quickly. We do have a few more days, don't we?"

She nodded. They had a week's grace, maybe more. Then it occurred to her that perhaps the baby wasn't the entire issue.

"You know, darling," she let her hand graze his arm as they walked toward the kitchen; "you know, it's not that dangerous, lots of women have them, and this man Suzy knows is excellent." But Murray's antagonism had nothing to do with his fear of the "abortionist," as he insisted on calling Suzy's doctor; no, his fear had to do with his feeling about destroying a perfectly good life. "Our life," he kept saying.

Still, Lise asked herself when she awoke later that night, was it so strange that a man who had spent his life working on genes would feel this way? She reached for some saltines and let them melt in her mouth. Her entire body had changed because of this new life swimming within her womb—each of its characteristics not even visible, yet fully formed. An infinitesimal blueprint for a completely new person. Murray was right: This tiny being growing inside of her wasn't two sets of anonymous chromosomes; no woman who had carried a child to term could believe that. She began to feel the deep pleasure at having created a new human being. And, she reminded herself, as she began to doze back into sleep, Murray had been a gentle-man. For not once during their talk had he said that it was she who had insisted on taking the chance that morning more than two months ago.

As the days passed Lise began to focus on the baby within her. She could feel herself moving more gingerly as the knowledge of what her body carried slowly imbedded itself in her brain. There was still time to make a decision. But what Lise didn't anticipate—what no one can ever anticipate—was the call that came that very afternoon to Murray's office while she and Diny were making a sandcastle in Riverside Park.

"Arthur's sick, Lise," Murray said when he scooped Diny into his arms. "We have to leave this afternoon. They've moved him to the hospital in Plattsburgh."

"That's not just sick," she protested on their way home, "not ordinary sick." Only when the door had clicked behind them, only when they were in their own home could he turn toward her and let her see the pain in his eyes. Only then could he take her into his arms and whisper, "They're not sure, darling, but they think it may be polio."

A Fascinating Case, 1954–1955

1

The stark, watery-green hospital room had been transformed into another world. Crammed with stuffed animals, toys, games, banks, flowers stuck into snippets of crockery and glass, pencils, crayons, paint, clay, drawing paper, books, even a small Victrola and records, it was the child's room at home scrunched into a smaller space so when he woke from his frequent naps he could forget for a few wonderful seconds where he was and why he was here. Amazingly, she had even managed to submerge the acrid hospital smell beneath the fragrance of the flowers and plants and the perfume she splashed on herself each morning.

When Arthur woke up, his mother was there, sitting within touching distance, her reddish-brown hair bent over the sweater she was knitting: a complicated ski sweater with white reindeer and two men on skis and snowflakes against a background of his now-favorite color, his camp color, which he had never heard of before this summer—copen blue.

She had bought the wool in a store on Seventy-second

Street the day Arthur arrived in New York by ambulance. He and twelve other campers had been cared for by kind strangers (no parents were allowed in the ambulance), and the saleswoman had asked how old he was, and how big, and Lise had pretended he was just like any other kid about to start school in a few weeks. She had not had to deal with the inexorable fact that Arthur was one of the unlucky ones who had gotten polio when there were only ten days left in the camp season, at a time when most people thought polio had been conquered.

That day in the knitting store was the last time she had felt like a normal person.

After that, Lise entered a world where time was suspended, where school was on another planet, where Diny existed most of the time only in the photograph she had hung exactly at Arthur's eye level across from the bed. Murray came every afternoon and evening, their pediatrician looked in every day, but so many others she knew and didn't know floated in and out of the room that their features melted into one surreal face. Even the other campers, whose names and parents she had learned so precisely at first, faded. They were wandering through the halls and playing Battleship and Monopoly; they were getting well.

Only Arthur languished in bed, too weak to leave the room while the doctors kept saying there was nothing to worry about; that for some reason they couldn't pinpoint but were not very concerned about, her child was recovering slightly more slowly than the rest.

"We're sure it's the milder form. We've taken blood and he has exactly what the others have, and they're all up and about, and soon he will be, too." Then the doctor would smile and his voice would drop into a confidential, coaxing, almost erotic tone. "So there's no reason why you can't go home and see your little girl. She must be missing you. The nurses in this hospital are the best in the city, Mrs. Branson, please trust them." Polite, discreet, kind, but essentially the message was: *Scram.* Get out of here with your worry, you're making everyone nervous, you're a bad influence on the floor, you've terrified the other parents, and you're not helping your child, either.

"But look at the patient," she would reply, "that's what Papa always said. Arthur's sick—the patient's sick, are you so blind that you can't see it?" she would shout while Murray's face blanched. Then another doctor would be called in—someone Murray had gone to school with, someone he had known in Boston, a superspecialist. Always the answer was the same: Be patient and your child will get well.

No one seemed able to understand that when she left the hospital, she was asphyxiated with anxiety; that the more she tried to "go about her business" (how she hated that phrase!), the harder she found it to breathe. That the minute she was out on the street, her brain became a reel of images: Arthur looking for her, calling for her, beginning to cry, his lips quivering slightly and his eyes welling up so they were more beautiful than usual. Or else she saw her child very still, scarily still. That when she came home to sleep or to see Diny, she spent the time poring over her old notes and journals to find everything she could on viruses, bacteria, bacteriophages, because something deep within her was telling her that, despite what they said, there was a twist here, a complication, what Murray used to call a "wrinkle" in the lab.

"How's Madame DeFarge?" the doctors greeted her. "Lise, darling, Liselotte, how are you managing?"

Her mother's worry crept through the phone wires when they spoke every few nights.

"Fine, Mama, coming along. The doctors say there's nothing to worry about, the tests are clean. It's just taking a little more time for him than the others. And you know how impatient I am," Lise lied, the words growing bitter on her tongue. Lies. Lies. Why was a life already filled with sickness also filled with lies?

"How're ya doing, kid?" Harry would walk into the room, his freshly shaven cheek brushing hers, his hankie poking out of his pressed pocket, his shirts pristine, his hair sleek. Such a contrast to Murray's rumpled weariness.

"Of course it's not your fault, it's nobody's fault, it happened," came from Rose's stony face, over and over again. But unsaid was: If only you had listened to us, sent him to *our* camp, the one *we* know.

With each visit, Lise's anger multiplied, as if Murray were responsible for his family. Lise had never held him responsible before, she had not had much to do with them. She knew she was being irrational, yet she didn't seem able to stop. And his answer, always the same, eminently reasonable, always gentle: "They mean well, darling, they don't want to hurt you. He can't say anything and she says too much, it's always been that way."

Suzy's misery, Stanley's guilt. Their boys had gone, scot-free, back to school. Every day one or both of them came, their hugs like vises, as if to convince themselves that their palms pressing against Lise's back could provide protection. Protection from what? Why should a child and his mother need anything that resembled protection if the child was getting well?

Then there was Diny's confusion when Lise came home, and, as time passed, her indifference to Arthur. "She hasn't seen him since the end of June and it's October," Murray rationalized. Besides, Nanny was back from her summer holiday and Aunt Rose appeared every few days to take Diny to the park or to the zoo or to Rumpelmayer's. So how dare Lise criticize Rose?

And Leo's detachment, his long-distance voice, wanting only the facts, what the doctors said, what Murray thought. No time to hear or ask what she was feeling. Oh, where is Leo, my lion? she wanted to scream as they talked. Yet it was good of him to call, he was busy, with a wife, two kids, problems of his own. "Just say the word and I'll be there, Lise," he would say. "Chin up, Lise, that's a good girl, and get some rest. You need it, with another one coming," he would caution her while she stood there, receiver in hand, defeated. What did he mean, be a good girl, when he knew perfectly well that she was a grown woman?

And always George. Every few days his lanky body would fill the doorway exactly as Murray's did, and Arthur's eyes would brighten. Together she and George would watch Arthur slowly open another Hardy Boys book, or a Terhune, or a Spike Jones record, a jigsaw puzzle, a miniature Erector set. After a week of no visits because George had a cold, Richard Halliburton's *Complete Book of Marvels,* and last, the same kite she had bought for Arthur when he was in camp. That did it.

"He woke up last night screaming and pointing to it," the nurse greeted her the next day. "This room must be cleared out, Mrs. Branson." Her voice was tight, exasperated.

"Just flowers," Lise instructed George, and each day she took something home with the promise, "It will be waiting for you in your room, darling."

But worst of all, Murray's resignation. "They're doing everything they can, Lise. This is one of the best hospitals in the country, in the world. And you have the baby to think about, and Diny, and me. Please, Lise, I beg you, come home in the afternoons and get the rest you need so badly . . ."

A week later, "You've lost so much weight and the nurses are wonderful there, and he is getting stronger. You can see the improvement, can't you? He'll never leave that room if you're always there. It would be better for him to be with the other kids, Lise. Are you listening, darling, please listen, Lise, please . . ."

Each time she nodded, ashamed for him that he had so easily been taken in by her lies. For she never admitted that she did rest in the afternoons, right there in the chair, a foot from where Arthur slept. Nor did she try to tell Murray the truth: Arthur was getting weaker, he slept longer and longer each afternoon. One of the reasons she stayed there with the door closed was that she couldn't let anyone see, that in some perverse way she needed to perpetuate the fiction that her child was improving. She did such a good job that Murray—the brilliant cell biologist whom she loved so much and who didn't, who couldn't, admit that his son, his firstborn child was dying—even Murray had been fooled. And for that she began to hate him and his need to believe her. She also hated his ability to reason logically, to function, to work, to continue to do all that needed to be done while Arthur was so sick. Murray was out in the world—where children no longer died of mysterious viruses—while she felt as if she were in a tunnel that existed in some era from the past, a tunnel that had no end and that narrowed with each passing hour.

But at least let Murray understand that she had to

be here, on guard, every moment, in case. Once she said it aloud, at the top of her lungs, while they were driving home, wondering why she was yelling at this man who never had trouble understanding her before—who, if anything, often knew what she was thinking before she said it.

"In case of what?"

She didn't know, but she had this foreboding, this dread that if she didn't stay with Arthur, if she didn't watch him eat and nap and draw and read, if she weren't there, she didn't know what might happen. So she pretended she didn't hear him and refused to meet his eyes.

Vainly, in her loneliness, Lise tried to keep a diary. If she could name her fears, maybe she could control them. Wasn't that what diaries were for? Wasn't that what her father had done with his diary of the 1930s in Europe? But all she could write were dry medical details: how much fever, what kind of medication, who saw him that day, what they said. After a few weeks she gave it up, merely scribbling, in her worst scrawl, the date, then *Arthur is alive*.

Only the knitting kept her calm. Now she was working on a sweater for Diny and next she would do hats, matching hats for herself and Murray. Sitting there, knitting, she could feel her world grow smaller and smaller. If the sun was very bright she would sometimes close her eyes and lean back into the stiff tweed of the chair and try to remember that morning at Lake Tear when she had felt transported into another world, a world that was a beginning, like a pinprick of light before it becomes a ray, then many rays arching across the sky. A world with rainbows and a soft breeze and molten light playing on water, and her and Murray's laughter. But then she would descend into this hermetic place lit by her child's feverish brown eyes that responded so completely to everything she said or read. After he went to sleep, though, Lise was totally alone, outside of time and space, where the very air was slower, quieter, colder, where objects seemed to be congealing in their places, where there was nothing to do but knit. And wait.

2

They sent him in the middle of October: a tall, prematurely white-haired man, nicely dressed, very correct and cool looking though the day was summer-warm.

"I'm Henry Farnsworth," he told her. "I'm a specialist in crisis intervention."

"I don't think I need a psychiatrist," Lise replied, amused. "I'm familiar with this disease, I've done work on viruses, and I also did some phage research when I was young." At that he smiled. She supposed she was still young to him, though there were days when she felt so old. "And I'm not one of those hysterical mothers who's afraid her child will be left with a polio limp. I was born in Europe, my father was a general practitioner, and I don't think everyone has to be perfect." Farnsworth looked at her with respect.

Then, as quickly as he had come, he was gone. Good riddance, Lise thought, but was pleased she had discharged that task with some aplomb. She didn't even attack Murray that evening. When he told her Farnsworth had been the pediatrician's idea, she believed him. A precaution. Okay. But finished. Done with.

At the beginning of November, Lise found herself daydreaming about Thanksgiving. Arthur propped at the head of the table, like some child out of Dickens, she thought ruefully, but tried not to brood. Instead she concentrated on the menu, who would be there, where she would seat them. With that in mind, she began to be more assiduous about Arthur's homework; after Thanksgiving there would be school.

"I'm getting to be a nut about the homework, it seems our one way out of the hospital," Lise confessed to Suzy. But Arthur didn't come home for Thanksgiving, nor did he go back to school. And suddenly there were stretches of time—sometimes ten minutes, sometimes as long as an hour—when he was distracted, unable to answer the simplest questions. In a panic Lise called the pediatrician.

"Don't jump the gun, Lise. He's probably developed a secondary infection that could make him tired and fuzzy. Take it easy, Lise." When the doctor came, Arthur was alert, relaxed, and answered all the questions perfectly. Lise gave a visible gasp of relief and felt like a fool.

But two days later, with no warning, Arthur developed a raging fever and complained of soreness in his joints. She held him in her arms while they stuck him for more blood, and more.

"It's the more virulent strain, Mrs. Branson, very rare, and not at all what the other kids had, you were right all along," the young resident confessed with awe in his eyes. Neither their doctor nor Murray had yet arrived.

When Lise watched them put Arthur into the iron lung, she could feel something in her brain begin to flicker, like the sudden crackling of a light bulb as it burns out. By the time Murray got in touch with Henry Farnsworth and met him at the hospital, what Farnsworth saw was not the delicately pretty, impeccably groomed, sweet-smelling woman he had talked to six weeks before. Instead, here was a distracted, unkempt creature who mingled her ordinary speech (at times quite lucid) with jarring nursery rhymes and tremulous, singsong questions like: "Did you know there are no calamities in Calamity Brook?" "Hudson had the last laugh on Emmons and Hall, didn't he?" "Where will the sins float to?" "Novaya Zemlya is where Rambout Van Dam met Alice in Wonderland, isn't it?" "Shall we have Verplanck Colvin or Tiny Tim for New Year's Eve?"

The nurse ushered them into the room and said, "She always loved to sing to him and carried a tune beautifully, but never like this. And she hasn't sat down for hours; since those test results came back, she's done nothing but pace and won't even look at food. She's going to wear herself to a frazzle—she's already worn to a frazzle. If she carries that baby to term it will be a miracle."

Murray pressed his lips together. The sicker the patient, the more freedom the nurses took. An old story. Then he fixed his eyes on Farnsworth's stunned face. The psychiatrist had been so sure they were all exaggerating. "It can't be," he had repeated several times on the telephone.

Well, now he could see for himself.

There was the reddish hair, the narrow frame, the expensive sweater and skirt, those pearls she wore like a talisman. But suddenly she seemed to need maternity clothes: Her skirt had come unbuttoned, and her pearls bounced on breasts that sagged (she must have loosened her bra), and her sweater was baggy what with all her pulling at it. Now she was kicking off her shoes, and in her stockinged feet she looked smaller than she was; compared to her thickening middle her ankles and wrists were twigs. In hours her entire appearance had changed; it was weird, uncanny, yet as he watched Farnsworth observing

Lise, Murray felt not only amazement but shame.

Shame that he hadn't listened more closely to her fears. He had abandoned her. That was why she was losing her mind. The proof was in her eyes. Staring out of her waxen face were eyes Murray had never seen before, eyes covered with cataracts of fear, their grayish-blue bleached to an unrecognizable no-color.

She didn't even know they were there. Since that initial high cry, like an animal caught in a trap, that had surged from her when she heard the test results, her entire being had focused on her child. As she circled the unwieldy iron tank whose roundness matched the roundness of her swelling body, she would bend toward Arthur's head, whisper something to him, graze his brow with her fingertips. When she seemed most desperate she would lunge toward him, giving all who watched a start—surely she wouldn't hurt the child?—and gently brush her lips across his caked, feverish mouth as if only she in this whole world could give him enough breath.

Now Farnsworth was muttering something to Murray about being Jewish. Were they observant? the doctor wanted to know.

"What?"

"Are you religious?" Farnsworth asked. Murray stared. "Do you believe in God?"

Murray shook his head. What use was it to talk of God? Surely Farnsworth could see that they had come too far for God?

Henry Farnsworth came to the hospital every morning but could do nothing. Lise wouldn't even make eye contact with him as she circled Arthur, walking miles each day. The nights were the worst. Her pacing was so rapid, so unnerving that the nurses began to complain. "She stalks him like a lioness," one would mutter whenever she saw Murray. But he pretended not to hear.

With each passing day, her behavior became more frightening. Her lips were seams, her face a mask, her eyes electric beams riveted to Arthur. The merest flicker in his face was enough to send her to the nurses' station, where her very presence demanded attention. Her manner had acquired an odd, harsh grace—no time for amenities, no time for anything but Arthur. The contrast between her concern for her sick child and her neglect of her unborn baby was so strange, so puzzling that everyone who saw her predicted that afterward she would simply lie down and give birth to a premature stillborn.

Lise astonished them all. After Arthur was pronounced dead in the middle of December—almost four months to the day that he was moved to the Plattsburgh hospital—of complications due to a rare and virulent virus somehow related to the polio virus (no one would ever know exactly because Lise wouldn't agree to an autopsy), she looked at Murray and said, "It's over, and there is nothing more I can do."

"She's going to be all right," Farnsworth told Murray. "She's a fascinating case, but she's going to be all right." Then he added that he wanted to see her once a week until the baby was born. "Just a precaution, one can't be too careful now."

"I did everything I could, Mama, honestly, everything," she said when she fell into her mother's arms.

"Of course you did, Liselotte, of course you did." Simone stroked Lise's hair and held her swollen body to her. She was stupefied by Lise's appearance. They had kept the madness from her, or she hadn't been listening hard enough, Simone now berated herself. Why hadn't she come? Then Simone heard those well-meaning echoes: "You mustn't put yourself through that, there's nothing you can do, she doesn't know anyone is alive but Arthur, we'll need you later." Leo, Emanuel, Murray, her friends—all wrong. She should have come. Mothers can put themselves through anything. Lise had, and she should have, too.

Lise didn't blame her mother for not coming, she didn't seem to blame anyone. She had been aware of her mother's concern and of Murray's sadness, she had seen Farnsworth and the doctors and nurses and even all those medical students gaping at her, but she hadn't known what to say. What could she say? There are no words when you are watching your child die.

So they had thought her mad.

Did it really matter? Let them think what they wanted. She didn't have the strength to dissuade them, to plead her case. For her firstborn, her inquisitive, precocious firstborn, the son she had named for her father, the Arthur she had expected to know for the rest of her life, was suddenly, incredibly, dead.

3

After Arthur died, Lise was suddenly responsible for another life: the baby she carried in her womb. She had scarcely been aware of that child while she cared for Arthur; now she realized that within three months she would have another child.

In what seemed like minutes she had been catapulted from the tunnel into the wide world again, a world with sky and horizon and colors besides that washed-out green of the hospital, a world with voices other than Arthur's whispers, a world with laughter and the noises of cars rushing and sirens yowling and buses stopping. A world with infinite possibilities.

Still, she could hardly feel anything. Only if she concentrated very hard could she hear what Diny or Murray or Nanny asked her, and only when it was dead quiet and she was alone could she feel the baby moving inside of her. It was as if she had brought that light green world that smelled of spoiling milk (now, finally, she could identify that horrible smell) into the real world, one superimposed on the other.

First to the funeral home, then back to the apartment, then to the funeral, and finally to the cemetery. Winter again in a cemetery, though this time the ground wasn't as frozen nor the air as bitter as it had been when her father died. Arthur's coffin looked so small, so forlorn; Lise stood there and wondered how she was ever going to forget it. Then she steeled her brain for the inevitable thuds of frozen earth as they hit the coffin and wondered vaguely if she would scream this time, but she realized that Murray had anticipated her. She saw one of the gravediggers drag a large bag toward the open grave; it was filled with damp, greenhouse soil. Everyone took a handful and placed it on the coffin, and after that they all left. No need to wait until the grave was filled in.

On the way back home, which went through Honeywell because of a new series of one-way streets, Lise noticed that the shutters of her old home were crooked, probably because of the bitter cold that had settled on them. But in her mind those crooked shutters became the sign that even the inanimate house somehow knew that Arthur Hurwitz's namesake had died. And it was always that strange image of the shutters that flew into Lise's mind when she remembered her son's funeral—the crooked shutters and Murray holding her, protecting her, never leaving her side until they arrived home, where Diny and Nanny were waiting for them.

After the endless week of *shiva,* Lise wooed sleep, and sleep rewarded her with a sweet dreamlessness that blanketed her from questions, answers, advice, cautions. A sleep as deep as the ocean at night, so deep that she had to struggle out of it each day, and in that struggle had a few seconds of freedom before she remembered that Arthur had died. But then it would come, the remembering, as menacing as a long roll of thunder over the river on a sticky August evening, and she would resist the temptation to lie down and seek sleep again and force herself to get up and go through the day with that noise of remembering in her ears. Sometimes it was dull, subsiding to the sound of a seashell, sometimes it was so loud she was sure she was going deaf.

Finally, she mentioned it to Henry Farnsworth. He nodded. "It may be a reflexive mechanism, for protection," he said. Lise stared. She didn't much like him, she thought he was what they called "thick" when she was a child, and she found him pedantic and too puritanical for her taste. Then he would come up with something so correct, like this. That's exactly what the noise was, protection against what everyone said: how well she was doing; how lucky that she was married, or pregnant, or financially secure; how fortunate she was to have Diny; how some husbands were killed by cars or planes or cancer or heart disease; how some children fell off horses and bicycles and became vegetables. The variations were endless and spoken in crooning, syrupy voices that could not quite hide their relief. Tragedy had touched someone else and was still passing them by.

It was easier to stay home. Lise began to play the piano again. Her mother came north for an extended visit. While Simone sewed, Lise played Mozart, Brahms, Bach, Debussy, Schubert. When she got to the second movement of the Appassionata, Simone breathed easier. Let her play, it was a good outlet, a release. Some days Lise felt possessed, yet she couldn't stop the thread of music. Steadily it grew stronger, until one day a neighbor stopped Murray to ask if his wife was changing careers.

At that Lise finally laughed, her old laugh that rippled across the coffee table and down the hall into Diny's room. The little girl came out to see what had happened, and Lise pulled her onto her disappearing lap. Murray sighed with relief, Nanny made herself another cup of tea, and later that evening Simone called Emanuel to say she was flying back to Florida.

Slowly Lise's cheeks filled out, her skin grew less pasty, her hair regained its old radiant sheen. No more was she that waiflike creature circling an iron lung. Despite the cold winter she was healthy again. "She's making real progress," Farnsworth reported in answer to Murray's weekly call.

Then, one day, Lise looked up at Dr. Farnsworth and said, "This seems too easy, doesn't it? Me coming for emotional sustenance, and you giving it?" Then she laughed her laugh that defied all the sound softeners in his office. But before Farnsworth could answer, she blurted, "I've been lying to you, I hardly touch Diny, only when someone is watching me. I feel as if I'm on stage, in a play, and every movment is calculated. Worse than that, I can't bear to have Murray come near me. We never make love, I've lied to you about that, about everything. How can I let him touch me when I'm tainted? How can I let him near me when I'm full of death?"

Farnsworth didn't know. But he did know that he had failed. He had sat here week after week and been taken in by intelligence, a sense of independence, and a lovely face. Not a striking, arrogant face, but a face whose beauty grows on you, a face not quite sure of itself. He had spent so much time watching the subtle planes of Lise Branson's face that he hadn't been listening as hard as he should have.

But the hour was over. He wrote a stern note to himself, and promised to talk to her about her questions next week.

Farnsworth never got the chance. Two days later, Lise Branson was hospitalized with a diagnosis of extreme paranoia, possibly latent schizophrenia. Within days she was ravaged, pale. Weight dropped off her body in handfuls; her bones seemed about to poke through her translucent skin; her eyes raced, wild.

"I can't understand it, it was sudden, so unexpected. She was doing so well," Murray said. Help me, help us! his eyes begged.

"Kill me, kill me before I have this child," Lise screamed each day in German when Farnsworth came. Sometimes she knelt at his feet and clutched his legs so hard that he had to call a nurse to help break the vise made by her rigid, unbelievably strong arms. Each day was worse than the one before. Days and days of that frantic screaming, her continual reciting of her childhood rhymes, her refusal to speak English or to see anyone's face. Day and night they watched her. Nurses came for a few days, then left, exhausted by her incessant ranting, her unwillingness to eat or be washed.

Murray called Simone. She came north again and put on a nurse's uniform and fed Lise and kept her clean and talked to her in German, "Liselotte, Liselotte darling, say hello to Mama," then read her yet another German fairy tale. Although Lise didn't resist Simone, she had no idea who her mother was. Not even when Simone held her in her arms and rocked her like a baby. "She's so cold, colder than the rings of Saturn," Simone would murmur to no one. For who could understand that old code of Arthur's, which he used for the patients who were very sick but whom he knew he could save: the boy who almost drowned, the man whose heart had stopped but whom they had revived, the small girl whose head had been burned by a pot of farina falling on it. "They were colder than the rings of Saturn," Arthur used to say, "but we brought them around."

The case looked hopeless, Farnsworth decided, surrounded by the growing terror in Simone Gray's eyes, the steady fear in Murray Branson's voice. Finally, he made a decision—he would see Lise one last time, then turn this difficult case over to a man he had known in medical school, a man he respected and sometimes envied. A wizard with paranoia and the rest of Lise's symptoms. Everything was arranged.

It was late February. New York was sighing restlessly under a blowy snowstorm. The world outside was as white as Lise's room, for she had spent the last six weeks destroying anything with a trace of color in it.

Murray was seated in a corner when Farnsworth arrived. Farnsworth had asked him to come, and, as usual, Lise did not acknowledge her husband's presence. Yet today she didn't lunge at Farnsworth when he entered, nor did she scream that high wail that was her usual greeting.

Today she sat very still in the chair near the bed; her face and eyes blanched to that no-color; her small, still shapely hands folded on her bony knees. When she spoke, her voice was a clear strand of sound.

"Good morning, Henry Farnsworth," she said in English, then forced her bluish lips into a dazzling smile. She rose and went to her husband, then kissed his cheek, as if she had not seen him for a few hours.

"It's a miracle," Murray insisted later. His face was haggard, yet his deep brown eyes glistened with triumph. "The most incredible thing I've seen, anyone's ever seen," he persisted over Farnsworth's attempt to convince him that Lise's recovery had been spontaneous and that not even he, the doctor, understood it.

Within days, Rose and Harry Branson sent the Farnsworths a Steuben owl. "To symbolize your wisdom," the note said. George Branson sent a book of Rubens's drawings for Mrs. Farnsworth, who was an artist, and Simone Gray presented Farnsworth with a leatherbound copy of Dante. He also received letters from several of the doctors who had cared for Arthur Branson and knew Lise and Murray. Friends told him Lise's obstetrician was calling him a genius, and the toughest nurses regarded him with new respect, bordering on awe.

"I feel like a fraud," Farnsworth confessed to his wife. "And I still don't know how it happened."

Lise had some idea. But how could she begin to describe the coldness, the harsh, shadowy denseness of that place where she had been exiled for these past six weeks? Two days after confessing the truth to Farnsworth, she had gone to Best & Co. to do some shopping for her new baby. She had walked through the familiar aisles, heard the tap of her heels on the well-worn wood floors, and just as she was about to engage a salesgirl in conversation, she felt as though the floor beneath her had opened. Swiftly she was dropped into a frigid, unfamiliar place with looming shadows and frozen, ghostlike figures. The entire experience had felt like minutes; she had been sure when she saw Murray and Mama sitting there and Dr. Farnsworth coming into the room that it was only minutes. For she had had the sensation that her lungs were filling, that her whole body was filling with the coldest substance she had ever known. And then, suddenly, she had been thrown out of that place that was even worse than the tunnel, bolted from it, but instead of finding herself in the infants' department at Best's, she had been in this glaring white place and huge flakes of snow were pelting down outside her window.

And it was over.

But six weeks! No one could live on the rings of Saturn for six weeks. So better not talk about it. She didn't want them thinking her crazy again. The best thing would be to keep her mouth shut.

Gilbert Arthur Branson was born on March 9, the Farnsworths' wedding anniversary. An easy delivery. Birth weight: eight pounds, ten ounces. Baby and mother well.

After that crucial day of the snowstorm, Lise never uttered another word in German. She could still understand it and read it, but she couldn't form the words to speak it aloud.

One of the first things she did upon arriving home with her new baby boy was to get her diary and correct it. "Arthur is TOT," she wrote on the day he died. Then she wrote "Arthur is TOT" ten or eleven times down the page. At the very bottom was one last entry: "Gil is a week old. Arthur is TOT." Yet now her handwriting was normal, firm, not that wavery hand she had had when her child was dying.

And her voice, too, was firm when she announced that evening to Murray, "I don't really believe in diaries, don't see much point to them. I've made one last entry in the one I started, and that's the end of it." As she spoke she could see Murray's face soften. How much he wanted to believe that her illness was over! How much she wanted to believe it herself!

As the months passed, their life together slowly found its way back to normalcy. But when Lise had the strength to admit it to herself, she knew that her life would never be the same again. She could never be that woman who had sat so peacefully, so tranquilly at Lake Tear less than a year ago, so sure of what she thought she knew, so convinced she could control her life. How naïve she had been, how innocent, how stupid! She had watched one child die and given birth to another. But, more than that, she had gone mad. From now on—who knew? Would she be able to work again? Would she be able to take care of her children properly? She didn't know. She was sure of so little, except one thing.

From now on she would be the watched and Murray would be her watcher. So would all the others who had witnessed her madness—the Bransons, her mother, their close friends, Farnsworth. Yet there were two people in her world who didn't know of it: her children, Diny and Gil. And they must never know. Of that, Lise was absolutely sure.

About a year after Lise Branson's remarkable recovery, Henry Farnsworth wrote a paper about her and the extraordinary course of her illness, beginning with the day that

Arthur became sick. He called it "Loss of Language." It became a classic in its field.

Diny, 1980

She came in and out of my young life like a migrating
bird. After that day in Grand Central, I always saw my
brother Arthur behind a blue felt band being herded away
to God knows where. At the end of the summer, they told
me Arthur was coming home. But he never did. And then
my mother went away and came back for brief moments,
usually when I was going to bed or getting up. I can still
smell her perfume as she bent over me, I can still feel those
smooth lustrous pearls as they grazed my arm. But after
a while those quick visits stopped, and I was told that
Arthur was dead, but I didn't think of him as dead—how
could I know what dead was?——no, I simply imagined
him walking away from us until all I could see was the
back of his head. Perhaps, in a childish way, I believed
that to die meant to disappear in the recesses of Grand
Central Station.

 The day she came back, my mother hugged me and
her eyes really seemed to see me. All I wanted that afternoon
was to sit forever in her lap. I could feel her heart beating,
and it reminded me of another day, a day that seemed very

long ago, when we had been making our fabulous sandcastle in the park and my father had suddenly appeared and carried me in his arms while he and my mother ran. I kept putting my hand on his heart, amazed by its rapid beat. Young as I was, I think I knew that something important was happening, and I could feel a shudder of fear surge through me.

Of course, I was right. Not long after that my mother left and then returned. She pulled me onto her lap, right next to her heart. Just as I was beginning to nestle against her, to smell her fragrant smoothness against me, she thrust me from her and before I knew what was happening I was on my feet, following her into her bedroom. There she stood on a chair, straining to reach a large box at the top of her closet. My father came into the room. As she was pulling what looked like a mammoth pillow from the top shelf he pleaded with her to come down. His voice was low. "Lise, Lise, darling, please come down, please stop this, you'll hurt yourself and the baby."

Who was he talking about? *I* was the baby, and she wasn't anywhere near me. I can still remember looking around the room, puzzled, trying to find the baby. It took years before I realized that the baby had been inside of her, the baby was Gil, and that my mother had gotten the idea that if she got the eiderdown from the closet and I slept under it I would be safe. That was the day my brother Arthur had died.

But then there were long afternoons on her lap when she seemed to have all the time in the world while she read to me, talked to me, taught me how to make an endless horse's rein with her left-over wool. And every night she tucked me into bed beneath the eiderdown. I slept under it for a while—how long I don't really know—

and then she and it disappeared, and when she returned, this time with a new baby, I was told I had another brother, named Gil.

It was all so confusing, that coming and going, brothers disappearing and appearing. Yet I was happy. For, now my mother was home for good.

Each afternoon when I came home from school, after we moved to Honeywell, she would be waiting, usually reading in the living room. When she looked up, her eyes a little startled as they made the transition from the page to me, I knew that she was happy to see me. Then she would take off her glasses and fold them into their case, and I would watch her thin fingers—long for such a small person—put her leather bookmark into her book and I would know that she was ready to listen to whatever I wanted to tell her. Gil and I would spend hours in the kitchen talking to her while she made dinner, and whatever had unnerved us during the day seemed to fall away in her calm, listening presence.

She had frightened us only once. But, by this time, it was so long ago we had forgotten about it.

We were about seven and three and still lived on Riverside Drive. It was a rainy day, more than a rainy day, perhaps a hurricane, for the rain beat at the windows and the river was angry with foam. Nanny was afraid to go out and had called to say she wasn't coming. We usually loved days like this: Often we would climb into our parents' huge bed and my mother would read to us about Mole or Mrs. Tiggy-Winkle or Alice. But today she seemed out of sorts, and her gestures were agitated, almost jerky.

She was standing on a chair again, reaching up into her closet, but my father wasn't there to warn her to be careful. Before Gil and I knew it, she had pulled a large box from the shelf and had put it on the floor. And then she was kneeling in front of the full-length mirror, pulling clothes from the box: pants and shirts and jackets and sweaters and pajamas. She would hold each piece up to Gil's chest, then pull some over his head and stand back to look at him. Considering. When she didn't like what something looked like she would pull the piece of clothing off Gil and put it on a pile she called "Charity." The other pile, the imaginary pile, for there weren't any clothes on it yet, was called "Gil."

Finally Gil asked, "Who's Charity," and I could feel my breath come again. His small voice had cut into the tension of that too-still room as clearly as a piece of shattering glass.

"Who's Charity?" he asked again, and that terrible silence was broken at last, and my mother's face began to look more normal as she pulled off the shirt she had insisted Gil wriggle over his head, even though anyone in his right mind could see that it was going to be too small for him. But when she had got it off him and he was still wincing with the tightness and pain, she began to cry. And cry and cry, as she crushed us both to her, crushing us so tightly I thought I was going to suffocate. Crushing us to her with those clothes that still had the marvelous smell of freshly laundered wash that has been dried in winter sunlight until it is almost frozen, then pulled off the line and folded before the smell of sun and cold and clean could seep from them. Whose clothes were they? How had they gotten there?

But there was no time for questions. Now the wonderful smell was gone, too, back into the box whose top my mother was carefully interlocking, as if she never intended to open it again; and while she was doing that, her face and wrists and hands were drenched with tears, and because she kept pulling us toward her, our hair and foreheads and chins were wet, too. And all the time she kept saying words that neither of us could understand or string together in any sensible way, even when we were older. But that day we knew that Charity had something to do with *idiots-and-fools* and *doctors-who-didn't-know-their-business* and *Arthur's-clothes-that-were-still-in-good-condition.*

But I didn't say anything to my father or Nanny. Something about my mother's eyes told me that this was our secret. Neither Gil nor I ever told.

New York, 1960

Lise hadn't known how she would manage when she came home with her new baby, but gradually she discovered that people are so involved with their own problems that they forget yours. Or at least they appear to forget.

Oddly, a few people, the ones who were closest to her in some ways, never held her madness against her. Murray. And her mother and Suzy and Nanny, who seemed to feel that any mother who loses a child is entitled to go crazy. Those three very different women conveyed, each in her own way, the feeling that whatever Lise had experienced was temporary and would pass. Never did they treat her in the least bit strangely.

Others weren't so generous, but they seemed to be forgetting. Oh, occasionally she would catch Rose or Harry staring at her with a worried question in their eyes, but Lise would quickly offer an excuse: a cold coming on, a sinus headache, that time of the month. Whenever George greeted her, he would unconsciously frown, but Lise soon learned to erase those lines between his brows by giving him her widest smile and stretching her arms out for a hug.

Even Murray seemed to have stopped watching her so carefully. He encouraged her to keep her appointments with Farnsworth—at first once a week, then twice a month, then once a month—but his initial solicitude, suffocating in its concern, had lessened, and sometimes he would even lose his temper at her. That was the best sign of all.

For Lise felt guilty not only about all that she had inflicted on him, but about his work, as well. He still wrote brilliant papers and was highly regarded by his colleagues, but the feeling she had when she went to meetings—unsaid, but still there—was that Murray had never quite fulfilled the promise he had shown when he was running Davison's lab. Occasionally she let herself wonder what he might have done if she had not been sick. But then she would dismiss it; besides, she wasn't sick anymore, and Farnsworth said it was futile to play the game of what-if. "It accomplishes nothing, Lise," he would say in a patient voice.

Going to work helped. In the lab three afternoons a week, Lise forgot who she was as she looked down the microscope or wrote up her data. Abe Goodside and the others were very kind when she first came back to work, and if they ever thought she behaved oddly, they gave no sign.

There were even days when she didn't think about Arthur, when those awful images of her child in the hospital would abate and she could forget that she had ever been mad. For Lise had only a slight recollection of those six weeks when she had retreated into her own world: faces coming and going, the cold, white room, Farnsworth's voice. Shame still filled her when she thought about not recognizing her mother, but Farnsworth said that, too, was futile. No one is expected to do penance forever.

And, most important, she was perfectly normal to her children. After that terrible day during the hurricane of 1958 when she had forced Gil into Arthur's clothes, she had had not one lapse. And Farnsworth had assured her that it probably had more to do with the drop in barometric pressure than anything else. No, she was sure they didn't suspect a thing. She played with them in the playground like any other mother, she read to them endlessly, she was teaching Diny how to play the piano, and she listened to Rose's and her mother's accusations that she was spoiling them with a knowing smile. She didn't care what anyone said. She would do exactly as she pleased where the children were concerned. She had earned that right.

Later, when they were both in school, she was the first to volunteer for any job that had to be done. She was recognized, she knew, as a model mother.

Lise was feeling so encouraged that she decided to give a party for Murray's forty-fifth birthday. After all, Gil was in kindergarten now, and it was time she did more than go to work and take care of the kids. Besides, there seemed no better way to express her gratitude to her husband, whose love for her never seemed to waver.

Everyone she had invited was coming. Leo and Norma and their twin girls. Simone. Once again her mother was a widow: Emanuel Gray had died of a heart attack a year ago, and now her mother was freer to travel. And Harry and Rose and George and his new wife, Joanna, and several of Murray's nieces and nephews and their wives and husbands were expected, as well. And, of course, friends from Murray's office and hers, too, and their close friends, the Cahns, the Hubers, and the rest.

On Friday, her day off, Lise walked leisurely from store to store, shopping for the party. She knew she didn't want to live as Suzy did, without any work of her own, attending meetings where people were convinced they could beautify Harlem or save New York from dog do or prevent the erection of tall buildings on the east side. But still, it was pleasant to be able to plan this party without the pressure of a full-time job. Yet she was moving so slowly. All the tasks she had relished when she was growing up and as a young married woman—cleaning the silver, arranging the flowers, figuring out where everyone would sit, setting out the food—seemed monumental. By evening, when she and Murray were on their way to La Guardia to pick up her mother, Lise's legs were rubber.

But the next morning she felt refreshed. Lying in bed she listened to her mother's singsong voice chattering with the children, then the familiar clank of the breakfast dishes, and beneath them, like the weakest voice in a fugue, the newscaster's voice while Murray shaved to the accompaniment of the radio. A lemon sun streamed through their bedroom; it was a glistening May day that you dream about when you plan a party.

By noon the table was set, and Murray had taken Diny and Gil to Nanny's apartment where they were going to spend the afternoon. The chicken tarragon was all assembled and refrigerated, a salmon mousse was jelling, trays of hors d'oeuvres were stacked in the tiny butler's pantry that had seemed a ridiculous luxury when they first saw the apartment but which was useful when they had guests. From the door to the kitchen, Lise could watch her mother surveying the living room, then plumping the pillows, arranging cigarettes and ashtrays, plucking dead blooms off the flowers.

Her mother had to be almost sixty-five, Lise realized, though you would never know it to look at her. Straight and regal, Mama was constantly taken for younger than she was. Still, Lise could see more lines around her mother's eyes and across that lovely high forehead, a slight hesitation in her walk because she was afraid of falling and refused to wear her glasses in public, and more liver spots on her expressive hands. Maybe Murray was right, maybe they should look for a really large apartment and ask Mama to live with them. When she mentioned it casually, while they were arranging some fruit, Mama shook her head.

"I never thought I'd get used to Palm Beach; you remember how unhappy I was at first. For years I used to dream about the Honeywell house, the garden." Her mother paused as she took off her glasses and stared toward the river. "But you can get used to anything, Lise—if I've learned nothing else in life I've learned that—and I have friends and the library, and the apartment is lovely. It's my home now, where I belong."

Later, when her mother sat down to do a hem on one of Lise's skirts (unbelievably they had finished all the chores early), Lise noticed how gray Mama's hair had become. A pang of apprehension filled her throat, but she dismissed it. She knew Mama was right. Every morning Simone went to the library to arrange a bouquet of flowers and set up the ongoing book sale. And she had her bridge games and the temple and her friends and her collection of rare shells. In Florida her mother had become independent; if she moved back to New York she would be merely Lise's mother or the children's grandmother.

But when Leo arrived and hugged Lise and whispered, "Mama's gotten old," Lise could feel her chest cavity fill with fear. She hurried to her room to get dressed, and while she was taking deep breaths to calm herself, Lise heard the children and Nanny arriving, and then Mama and Leo and Norma oohing and aahing over them. Quickly she slipped into her dress and rubbed some rouge onto her cheeks. The mascara and eye shadow made her gray eyes darker—"smudged," Murray said, because he didn't see why she needed to do anything to her face, but she felt better with a little makeup on. Oh, why did I undertake this party? Whatever possessed me? she wondered as she hurried toward the living room.

When he saw her, Murray stared. "Oh, Lise, oh my darling," his voice was so tender it almost hurt her to hear it. "Lise, you've got your dress on backwards," he whispered, then propelled her back to their room. She looked down. Oh, my God!

But at least the children hadn't seen, Lise consoled herself. Thank God the children hadn't seen.

Faces blend together like Dali's melting clocks as she wends her way through them, greeting the adults, settling the children, making certain everyone has a drink and pleasant conversation nearby. The perfect hostess, Lise thinks as she feels her lips form one smile after another and hears her voice rise in greeting. All of them have come to celebrate Murray's birthday and from their faces, their eyes, she knows she looks all right, but, strangely, something is happening to them. On Abe Goodside's square, somewhat stocky shoulders is Papa's bearded profile, actually frowning at her, puzzled perhaps as to why he is here. And instead of Gil's scrubbed and shining face, which he tilts upward every now and then to be kissed by yet another relative, is Arthur's ashen, wan one. She can hear her mother's voice trilling through the warm May air, and occasionally her laugh, yet where are the cousins? Sally, and Anna and Charlotte? And this girl Joanna? How did she get here? Who is she?

Lise can't understand it, this dizzying confusion that has overtaken her, so she slips back into her bedroom and takes the time to search her face in the mirror. Same face, not many lines, she's lucky—Mama's skin. Same face, but why these strange, unwanted images rushing through her brain when she least has time for them? She splashes cold water on her face and arms, then carefully, as if she has all the time in the world, applies more makeup and darkens her eyebrows slightly. Maybe that will do it; maybe if my face is on straight other things will fall into place, she decides. Then she walks as confidently as she can into the kitchen. The help is replenishing the trays.

"Everything's fine, plenty of everything, and just delicious, Mrs. Branson. What a good cook you are! Now don't you worry about a thing, you go out there and enjoy yourself," the woman in charge urges.

"Lise, Liselotte, do you want to hear the strangest thing?" Mama says. "Dr. Goodside knew Papa. They met at a conference once. Isn't this a small crazy world?" Mama's arm is around Lise's shoulders now, and Lise is engulfed by the sensation of her mother's body, the smell, that special blue-bottled fragrance—does it still come in blue bottles?—and suddenly it is as though a piece of her mind has given way, as if a rush of floodwater has broken the dam she so carefully built within it. She remembers her mother rocking her patiently, so patiently rocking her and singing to her, but she isn't little nor is she in Vienna or Honeywell: They are in an all-white room and Mama looks like a nurse and she is holding Lise on her lap and singing to her, but Lise has no idea where they are, and all she can do is see it in front of her, like a motion picture that someone starts to show before the room is completely dark, not-yet-focused figures with pale sepia edges mingling with the figures in the room.

Almost faint with terror, Lise leans into her mother's body and Mama bends toward her and whispers, "And how much he reminds me of Papa, your Dr. Goodside, it's uncanny, isn't it, darling? No wonder you're so fond of him." Then Lise is back in her New York living room, at Murray's party, and when she feels stronger she moves off to another group of guests, avoiding Rose's sharp blue ones, afraid that they will see more than she wants to reveal.

To give herself a moment to breathe, Lise stops in front of Diny and kneels down and straightens the bow on the little girl's middy dress; then she tucks a curl of Diny's red hair back into the barrette. Thick, wonderful hair, redder than Lise's ever was, more like Papa's, Lise imagines. Then, thank God, Gil's face is his own unblemished one when he approaches, wanting his own little show of attention from her.

There, that's better. Much better. And now she's almost at the other side of the room with the Bransons, and of course she recognizes Joanna—she's George's new wife and a terrific girl, too; only a little bit taller than Lise so Lise feels comfortable with her. Joanna reminds Lise of herself when she first met the Bransons; she's as nervous as Lise once was. But it's safer here, here there aren't as many memories, and she can make harmless chatter— which is what people are supposed to do at parties, isn't it? Now they're all admiring the river: Sometimes it's as dark as the blue wool crepe of Aunt Gertrude's suit, but today it's a piece of teal taffeta, a beautiful piece of teal taffeta that Mama used for Lise's dress to the eighth-grade dance.

Then she feels that peculiar movement in her brain

again, as if something has been let loose, and before she knows it she's telling them about Henry Hudson. He was her father's favorite so she can't understand why Papa is frowning at her again. Maybe he'll stop frowning if she tells them about Hudson, if she assures him she can still remember the details of that sad life . . .

"You know, it's the strangest thing," Lise begins, "Hudson appeared in history from 1607 to 1611 and no one knows where he was born. He found the river on his third trip for the Dutch East India Company and landed on Staten Island, traded with the Indians, and sent a boat north. The Indians attacked the boat in the Narrows, and a man was killed by an arrow through his throat. Then Hudson invited the Indians to trade some more and lured two onto his ship and took them as hostages. After a few days he sailed north to Castleton, and then he realized he hadn't found the Northwest Passage at all."

She shrugs and notices that Papa is still frowning. She puts her hand on his arm. Once he hears the end of the story, once he knows she remembers it so well, he will be happy.

"Hudson made one more voyage in search of the Passage, on the *Discovery* in April 1610. He entered Hudson Bay in August and early in November the ship went into winter quarters in James Bay. But then they became frozen in, and conditions grew terrible: sickness, shortage of food, discontent. A mutiny began and many of Hudson's loyal sailors joined it, including Robert Juet, who had kept Hudson's log when he discovered the river three years earlier with the *Half Moon*. As soon as the ice thawed, the mutinous sailors put Hudson and his son and a few others who had remained fiercely loyal into a small boat and abandoned them. No one ever heard from Hudson again, but the *Discovery* made it back to England. When there was a trial for Hudson's murder, all the leaders of the mutiny were acquitted."

Now she is finished, and her eyes are brimming because that part of the story always made her cry. Lise looks for Papa's face. But he is gone now, and Dr. Goodside and his wife are standing next to her, smiling, and behind them Lise can hear Rose say, "Lise is certainly an encyclopedia about that river, isn't she? One of these days she ought to write a book about the Hudson."

A few weeks after the party, Lise and Murray went to see Dr. Farnsworth and together they decided that instead of looking for a larger apartment in Manhattan, Lise might feel more comfortable if they moved to Honeywell.

Hearts-ease, 1965

Simone never approved of the decision to move back to Honeywell. "Why?" she kept asking when Lise told her about it. "Why go back to the past? You're still so young, you have all your life ahead of you, why go back to that town?"

Lise had all the answers. She wanted to bring up the children in the suburbs; she was sick of the city; she had decided not to work for a while, at least until the kids were older (she wasn't really accomplishing much on a part-time basis, you couldn't, really); she needed more air and light; the Honeywell schools were still good; and Henry Farnsworth lived twenty minutes north, in Scarborough Manor.

Simone was not convinced. You can't recapture the past, she insisted. Not even Proust could do that. She shook her head and wrote letters to Lise, to Leo, to Murray, even to Rose and Harry Branson. Of course, she regretted the last, especially when she received a very formal note from Rose, written on Tiffany stationery, declaring that she, too, thought Lise and Murray were crazy.

Although it was hard to keep resisting her mother's objections, Lise knew she and Murray were right. Honeywell was the place for them, and it wasn't as if they were going to move back to the house—no, that was impossible. It had been sold by the Goulds and was now a two-family affair, very run-down and hardly worth fixing up, even if they could talk the families into selling. Besides, it was much too big. No, she and Murray were not trying to recapture her past by buying her old house; they were looking at the newer houses, up on the hill, in the fancier section of town, with clear, long views of the river and the Palisades. Houses built right after World War II, with more conveniences and yet surrounded by some of the old oaks and maples that a smart builder had had the sense to leave. The one they found had a few custom details: cedar closets and wide fir floors that had been refinished a few times and gave the house a comfortable, lived-in feeling.

In the end, it was a good thing. Murray didn't mind the commuting nearly as much as everyone had predicted. As a matter of fact, he enjoyed it, and soon he was as enthusiastic a fan of the river as Lise. The schools were good and easy to get to; there was a terrific library and the garden club still met; there were local concerts and lots of people to play chamber music with, if Lise should wish.

Lise didn't miss the noise of the city, the smell, the dirt, or even her job. I'll go back to it in a few years, she told herself. And even though she missed Suzy desperately at first, Lise knew that she wouldn't be seeing that much of Suzy even if they still lived in New York, for Suzy had surprised everyone and gone back to law school. In Honeywell she would make new friends; people were so warm, especially the ones who remembered her family from the old days. Why, some of the women would stop her in the supermarket to tell her how much they still missed her father. "There has never been another doctor like him anywhere around here," they would say wistfully, while Lise patted their arms and comforted them.

Honeywell also seemed a better place to live now that the civil rights demonstrations and peace marches were in full swing. Lise smiled when she thought about it. In some ways she had moved here for the same reasons as her parents—not that you could escape Vietnam or the civil rights struggle anywhere. But, somehow, it felt safer here.

And she had discovered she was braver than she thought. She had actually played the piano for the eighth-grade production of *Anything Goes* because Diny had a lead part. As a result of that, she had had some invitations to play with a chorus and a quintet, and she was practicing the piano every day. So, perhaps it was better if she stayed home and took care of the house and the kids and wasn't dependent on help anymore. Nanny had retired when they moved from the city. And in some ways the kids seemed to need their mother more as they got older. She was ready for this sabbatical. And even Mama stopped nagging her when she heard that Lise was playing the piano again.

The summer of 1965 was hot and dry. Clouds of dust swirled around their ankles wherever they walked; forest fire warnings dotted the trees on the trails. At the beginning of August, Lise heard from a neighbor that a developer had bought the corner of Main Street where her old home still sat and was planning to tear it down and build an A & P. For days she was in a daze, berating herself that she hadn't persisted with Murray when they were looking for a house five years ago. If they had bought the house, the bulldozers and backhoes wouldn't be surrounding it now.

Murray saw Lise's sadness and reminded her how an architect friend had walked around the house with them. "Even from the outside he had seen a tremendous number of problems, you remember that, Lise. It wasn't worth it, darling. We would have been throwing good money after bad, even if we had gotten it for a good price. Do you know what it costs to heat a house that size?"

Of course, she knew. She remembered Papa shoveling coal into the fireplace on those black winter mornings, she remembered getting into her clothes under the eiderdown so her skin didn't prickle and tighten in the raw, dense cold of the bedroom when she jumped out of bed. She still hated to get out of bed in the winter and blamed it on those freezing rooms of her adolescent years in the Honeywell house. But still, how she hated the prospect of seeing the house destroyed.

Yet there was nothing she could do. And when they returned from their yearly vacation on Cape Cod at the end of the summer, part of the house—the porch and one turret—had already been demolished. Lise felt a catch in her throat every time she passed the old place, and she was glad when her neighbor, Doris, suggested they have a ladies' day in New York and go to the Metropolitan Museum.

The September day was as sticky as an August afternoon, but the train ride home had refreshed her, and when Lise got back to the house she decided to plant some bulbs before going inside to make dinner. Most women would have taken off that pretty dress before going to the garden, but Lise never wore gardening clothes or cleaning clothes. She simply did what needed to be done and worried about her clothes and shoes later.

When Diny came home from school, Lise stood near the garden shed, a trowel in her hand, her reddish hair mussed. Her forehead and one side of her dress were slightly smudged, and a cloud of dust surrounded her, giving her an odd halo. The earth was as hard as baked clay because of the drought.

"Over here, darling," she called and waved as Diny approached. From Diny's expression, Lise knew that all Diny wanted was to go upstairs and shed her clothes, drenched with perspiration, and jump into the shower. Diny offered her cheek for a kiss, though, then asked, "Putting in bulbs?"

"No, I have to go to the Gould house. I made a bed for the hearts-ease, in the corner, under the maple. You know Grandma planted it when I was a girl, about a year after we came here. We made a special trip up county to get it, and I can't let it die. Not now, not after all these years. They're tearing it down, the Gould house, I saw them when Doris and I came up the hill." Lise knew her eyes must look miserable. And her sentences had no flow. But she felt compelled to go on.

"They're tearing it apart." Her voice quivered and she looked at Diny, as if now, at the eleventh hour, she and her daughter might somehow prevent the destruction of the house. But, of course, they couldn't. Besides, they had been over this dozens of times, most recently when they were on vacation at the Cape. She had assured Murray and Diny and Gil, more than once, that she was prepared. So why am I behaving in this strange, erratic way? Lise asked herself as she watched Diny's bewildered face.

"Maybe it would be best to go to the house and stand

there and watch the wrecking ball slam into the old boards and walls and beams," Lise then ventured. "Maybe I had better confront it." She sounded like Henry Farnsworth now, but Diny's eyes brightened and she had stopped looking at her mother in such a puzzled way. Lise sighed while she waited for Diny to drop her books in the front hall.

But they never got to the Gould house. Maybe it would have been too painful to stand there and watch the wrecking, maybe they were each protecting themselves unconsciously—Lise from the sight of the house being destroyed and Diny from having to watch the pain on her mother's face.

For, once they were in the village, Lise remembered that she had to pick up some things before dinner: fish from Andrew's and a prescription for Gil's allergies from Michael's Drugs and bread, and somehow an hour flew by. All the while, they kept hearing the vibrations from the demolition equipment up at the old house, but just when they would have started to head for those odd reverberations, so unfamiliar on the main streets of this still sleepy village, Lise announced that she had to get home.

Besides, what was there to see? And didn't Diny know that Daddy was coming home a little early tonight, that he had a meeting? No, there was no time for anything else, she must head up the hill to start dinner.

Diny didn't argue. It was still so hot, and by now there was no longer any noise. A sudden silence seemed to fill the air. The wreckers must have gone home. Silently, the two of them trudged up the hill. It was then that Lise realized she had been scurrying through Honeywell with a muddy trowel hanging from her hand. What had people thought as they had watched them? And worse yet, what did Diny think?

At dinner Lise didn't say a word about the old house. She was planning to mention the noise of the demolition and her feelings about it, but somehow she didn't. No use upsetting Diny any more. Diny hated it when she got nervous, both children did. It usually happened when they were sick, but now, thank goodness, they were older and hardly ever sick. Still, it was better to keep the conversation light, cheerful.

When it was time to kiss Gil goodnight, Lise passed Diny's open door. Diny was doing her homework, turning the pages of her books against the hum of her parents' voices and the music playing in the background. Such a comforting sound, Lise thought: parents' voices meandering through their day, reporting, analyzing, discussing. She had loved to listen to her own parents' voices, even when they occasionally argued.

It turned out that Murray had no meeting tonight; Lise had been wrong. So it was a pleasant, long evening as they read and listened to Mozart against the sounds of the katydids and the occasional hoot of a barge on the river. Sometimes when it was as warm as tonight, they would take a walk down to the river. But Lise was exhausted and she knew Diny was, too. It wouldn't be fair to ask her to stay up and babysit while they went out. So, around ten-thirty, they began to shut out the lights and close the doors and soon there was the dull roar of the dishwasher as they went up the stairs.

Diny was already asleep, her clothes in a little heap near her bed. Lise gathered them and put them into the hamper. She had probably been too tired even to brush her teeth. Lise smiled. At fourteen Diny was now old enough to know that nothing would happen to you if you went to bed without brushing your teeth.

After he and Lise had been asleep for a few hours, Murray inexplicably became aware that Lise was gone. Almost in slow motion he put his feet on the floor—colder than he expected—and let his eyes accustom themselves to the dark, trying to organize his thoughts as he moved. He began by searching for the giveaway light that would tell him she was in the bathroom or checking the windows and doors downstairs or just standing in Gil's or Diny's doorway watching the children sleep. But the house was a thick, dark brown. Lise wasn't in it.

The garden. Perhaps she couldn't sleep—it was still humid, though a breeze was beginning to blow—and was wandering around the garden. Her mother used to do that when Lise was a girl; even now Simone insisted she got her best ideas for gardening at night, and perhaps Lise was figuring out where to plant her bulbs. Murray pulled some khakis over his pajamas and went outside. Inadvertently, he let the screen door from the kitchen slam, but when he paused, waiting for some sign that Diny or Gil might have heard, there was nothing.

No sign, either, of Lise in the garden. Furtively, Murray beamed his flashlight into all the corners, absently noting the bed she had dug up that afternoon. Then he went inside for his windbreaker and his keys and quickly backed out the car.

Slowly he cruised down to the river and back up Main Street. When he saw the bulldozing equipment, he knew, and after he had parked and wound his way around the trucks and debris, he saw her—a tiny figure in her white batiste nightgown kneeling under the large maple that seemed to be the only tree still standing in Simone's garden. She was furiously digging up some plants that she cradled to her chest after she had gotten them out of the ground, as if to reassure them that the trip wouldn't be too bad, and then carefully arranged them in the yellow bucket she had remembered to bring with her.

"I had to get the hearts-ease I wanted before they come in the morning. Otherwise it will be gone," she told him after he was almost on top of her. As if it were broad daylight and she were dressed properly. In the thin moonlight, Murray could see the dirt that had streaked her nightgown and the gooseflesh that was sprouting on her childlike arms.

He shook his head, but knew better than to get angry and simply waited until she had finished and stood up, rubbing the small of her back as she always did when she had done heavy work. Then they walked quickly, silently, to the car.

"No one saw me," she told him gravely, as if that would make it all right—her running down the hill in nothing but a nightgown and slippers, carrying her trowel and bucket, at almost two in the morning. As if she hadn't had almost five years to get the goddamned hearts-ease!

Murray didn't answer. When they got home, he tried to urge her to put water in the bucket and let the plants wait till morning. "Please come in and clean up and come back to bed," he whispered.

That was when she started to cry.

As soon as he heard Lise's small, scuffling cry and saw the extreme concentration of her body on the task at hand, Murray knew that there was no point in trying to convince her. She would never listen to him. He walked toward her, then stood over her as she went through the plants in the bucket, trying to find the one she would put in first, refusing to let him help her beyond holding the flashlight. Then she knelt and spread the roots of the hearts-ease and patted the earth, as if in prayer that the plants wouldn't die.

"They're very rare around here, you never see them except on the trails or in the woods. That's where Mama found them, and that's where we went to get them. And Mama had to ask dozens of people before she found out what they were called. I've wanted to do this for months. I was going to do it last spring, after Malcolm X was killed, but I forgot, and now it's almost too late." Her voice was high as it always was when she was tired or upset, yet it got a little stronger as she patted the last plant in and, finally, they could go to bed.

What Murray couldn't see as he concentrated on Lise was Diny standing at the upstairs window, staring down at them. But Lise had observed Diny; once when her glance swept the circumference of the garden, her eyes had lifted to the pastel, almost spectral figure of their child, watching, listening. She would have to figure out something to say to Diny, some way to explain finding your parents in the garden at three o'clock in the morning.

So the next day Lise made a point of telling the story of how she went with Mama to get the hearts-ease, even though Diny had heard it many times before. As she watched Diny's cautious, almost wary eyes, Lise wished she could gather that slightly awkward fourteen-year-old body into her arms and blurt out the truth: how the bulldozers had aroused memories and fears she didn't even know she still had—of her aunts' houses in Vienna, of the Nazis marching into those houses and destroying not only them but all the things and people in them. That the sight of her old home being leveled had taken her back to Pertisau and Vienna and her own adolescence in Honeywell and Papa's bloody map and the apprehension she sometimes felt when he read his beloved Rilke aloud. Or how she sometimes felt like that caged panther in Papa's favorite poem. "As he paces in cramped circles, over and over,/the movement of his powerful soft strides/is like a ritual dance around a center/in which a mighty will stands paralyzed."

No, you can't tell things like that to a teenage daughter who thinks you're perfectly fine. And if you can't indulge yourself, you will be perfectly fine. Doesn't Henry say that all the time?

So Lise assuaged herself and Diny with another kind of memory, a harmless family story. When Diny giggled at the part where Lise woke up and found Grandma snoring, Lise felt her body fill with euphoric relief. After that she made a determined effort to get out of the house. She needed to be less self-absorbed, she told herself, and within a few weeks she began to play the piano for a local chamber music group.

Valentine's Day, 1968, 1969

When Lise watched Murray come up the front walk, she knew he had news. Real news. His step was quicker than usual, and his long limbs suppressed a nervous excitement. She had seen that same energy when they were young, when they got some unusual, fascinating results on a lab experiment. She had also seen it a few times after they moved to Honeywell. But she didn't think she had seen it since all that brouhaha over Watson and Crick winning a Nobel prize. Lise wasn't sure. Some days she wasn't sure of anything; the years seemed to kaleidoscope into each other and time became blurred, muffled in her memory. Yet now, as she offered her upturned face for a greeting kiss, she knew that he was happier than he had been for a while. Something important had happened at work. It would have to wait, though, until they had opened their Valentine presents.

Valentine's Day had become an abiding tradition in the Branson house. Lise didn't really know why. Her parents had never celebrated it; it was a Catholic holiday, after all. But from the first year of their marriage, it had been

Murray's holiday, the occasion when he would come home with gifts for her and, later, for the children as well. It was touching—her husband of more than twenty years taking Valentine's Day as seriously as a young man courting his first love. Once Lise said so, and he had smiled and answered, "I am still courting my first love."

She knew she didn't deserve it. She had put him through so much in the years since Arthur's death. She knew his family thought his work had suffered because of her, and she had tried to discuss it with him more than once. But he always dismissed such ideas; when the Nobel prize went to the Englishmen, his answer was: "It was a race, and they won, as simple as that." But might it have been different if she had been different? Might he not have achieved more professionally? Might she have helped him? But when her thoughts went in that direction, Lise knew she was romanticizing: she and Murray were not latter-day Curies; even when she was young, back in the Boston lab, she had not indulged herself with such fantasies. For they were absurd.

This Valentine's Day Murray had outdone himself. A wine-colored cashmere sweater for Diny and a Swiss-made set of binoculars for Gil, who had become an avid bird watcher. And for her there was the brown Coach bag she had admired when they were window-shopping along Madison Avenue a few weeks before.

Inside the bag was more than the usual dollar bill and small change that the Bransons always put into gifts that carried money. Inside this new handbag was also a folded piece of thick paper. When Lise spread it before her, she saw it was a map. A map of Japan. Kyoto was outlined in red.

"I've been invited to be the keynote speaker at a

conference there next year," Murray said. His voice was low, but his eyes glistened. "Will you come?"

Lise looked around the table at the white cloth and the silver and crystal and the red napkins and candles that she always used on Valentine's Day. And their two children: Diny with her red hair and grayish eyes and exquisite fair skin, and Gil with his dark hair and eyes, like his father. They were sixteen and almost thirteen. Their eyes were expectant; they were old enough to know that their parents were very protective, perhaps a little odd, for Lise and Murray never went away without them and never sent them on trips or to camp. Yes, they knew that there had been an older brother who had died because of a virus he had gotten at camp, but that was ages ago. Although Diny remembered Arthur, he was somewhat remote to her, like someone out of a fairy tale. "I remember how proud he was of his new Mickey Mouse watch," Diny had once told Lise. They had bought it for him before he went to camp, and he died with it on his wrist. It was upstairs in Lise's top drawer. But beyond that, not much.

Now the children and Murray were waiting for her to say something. This was the test. Were they old enough to be left in Honeywell while she accompanied their father on this important trip to Japan? From their expressions, Lise could see they wanted her to go. They wanted to know she could live without them. Her need for them was becoming their burden.

"Of course I'll go, I'd love to go, why on earth wouldn't I go?" Lise heard herself say. Murray looked at her sharply. He doesn't believe me, she thought, but then as she listened to her voice she realized why he was observing her so apprehensively. Her voice had become very high and was lurching dangerously, as it always did when she was frightened. It sounded reckless, almost cavalier, not at all like her normal voice. She could see that it was beginning to unnerve the children.

So Lise became very silent as they ate and Murray told them what he knew about the trip. As he spoke, Lise could see how much this trip meant to him.

In the ensuing months, she tried to fathom why she was so afraid to go to Japan with him. Sometimes she thought it had nothing to do with their personal situation, but rather with her fright at what was happening around them. The spring of 1968 was even worse than the end of 1963. With King's death and then Robert Kennedy's assassination, the country seemed to have descended into a cave of death. Public fears had to exaggerate private ones, Lise felt.

If she could give herself a little time, perhaps as the months passed, she would be able to figure out a way to feel comfortable enough to go. She was grateful to Murray for giving her plenty of warning, and although he knew how afraid she was, he had reassured her over and over again that somehow she would come with him.

The children were getting older. Every few months Lise saw changes. By next spring Diny would be a senior in high school, seventeen years, a young lady. And Gil would be fourteen. Hardly a baby. Her mother had offered to come north and stay with them for the month that she and Murray would be away.

"Go, Lise, it's time you and Murray had a vacation by yourselves," Mama had said on the telephone at least five times. In her mother's voice was more than a little impatience. "You and Murray don't have forever, you know," she actually said once. In the last few years she had become critical of Lise's need to be so close to the children; she thought Diny should have gone on a summer trip, or even to camp as she was growing older, and Mama had told Lise more than once she was afraid Gil would become a mama's boy. But Lise had stubbornly rejected all her mother's suggestions. She had to see the children every day, she couldn't bear not checking them before she went to bed, watching their innocent sleep.

"What will you do when Diny goes off to college?" Henry Farnsworth had asked her several times these last few months. Lise didn't answer. She couldn't even bear to think about it.

The summer passed, and soon it was fall, a brilliant warm fall when the October light bent and stretched in ways Lise had never seen before. Sparkling, gorgeous light. The shimmering reflection of the foliage on the extraordinarily calm river made her heart lift. Not even the predictions among the Honeywell old-timers could dampen her spirits. "It's going to be a cold winter, the coldest in years," they warned. "That's what this still river means, gathering warmth for the cold winter."

When her mother came north for her usual few weeks from Thanksgiving through New Year's, Lise was almost convinced she would go to Japan. They began to shop for clothes for the trip, and when they went to the Bransons', as usual, for Thanksgiving, Rose was unusually cordial. "It will be wonderful, getting away together. It keeps a marriage fresh." Leave it to Rose to refer to their marriage as if it were a head of lettuce. Even Murray was amused.

But he didn't push her. This was her decision. No one could make it for her.

After Simone went back to Florida, the excitement began to build, and by the first week of February, Lise could feel it tightening around her like a vise. They would be away when Diny would hear from colleges, they would miss the senior play—how could they leave her during this crucial spring of her senior year? Yet Diny kept saying she would manage. "I'll be fine," she would reply defiantly. Lise was still uncertain. Then there was also her usual fear about flying. Even after they had gone to the lawyer to update their will, Lise began to have nightmares about flying together with Murray. Farnsworth suggested that they make arrangements to fly separately. That was when Lise realized she didn't have the strength, the nerve, the guts—whatever you wanted to call it—to go. She was still too afraid.

When she told him, Murray shrugged and smiled ruefully. "You gave it a good try," he said quietly. That was all. It was as if he had never really thought she would do it. She felt miserable: a fraud.

Even worse was the children's anger.

"You promised!" Diny repeated several times and looked at her with scorn.

"I know. But I can't. I just can't," Lise told her, then reached out to touch her. But Diny backed away, still furious.

Even Gil, that sunny, easy child, was upset. "You still think we're babies, you're still treating us like babies. When will you stop doing that to us?" he wanted to know. But in his eyes was also the question: When will you stop doing this to yourself?

On Valentine's Day, Murray brought home extravagant presents: luggage for Diny, a camera for Gil, a cameo for Lise. After dinner they had a family conference. Lise looked around the same table she had looked around a year before, yet now she felt hollow with disappointment. Why couldn't she do this? Why was she causing such pain on her children's faces? Why was she behaving like an invalid? Her throat thickened as she listened to Murray.

"It's not fair to ask someone to do what they can't do, and Mommy can't go," he began. "Her reasons are hers, and they are very special." Lise could feel her heart quicken. Was he going to tell them the truth? Her history? Her madness? Was he going to exchange their anger for their pity? Her glance shot from his face to Diny's, then to Gil's. They both dropped their eyes. Her eyes filled; neither of them had ever treated her like this before.

But of course Murray wasn't going to betray her. How could she have considered such a thing? No, he was merely talking his way out of a tight spot, and as she listened to him, Lise felt like a child, a problem child. Now he was talking about her as if she weren't here—he had never done that before—but she couldn't get angry. How could she get angry at someone for being so understanding, so kind?

"You can't throw someone who is afraid to learn how to swim into a pool and expect him to make his way," he was saying. "That's cruel, and it would be cruel of us to expect Mommy to do something that creates so much anxiety in her that she's miserable. Besides, it will be nice to have her here for the senior play and when those letters from the colleges arrive, Diny. The timing wasn't very good for this trip. When I came home last year, I didn't think it through properly. And she'll be here when you're preparing for your exams, Gil; that first round of exams in high school is no joke." His voice was smooth, assured. Then Murray looked at Lise. "And you do want to work in the garden, get the place ready for summer. And there wll be other conferences, lots of conferences," he lied and gave her a cheerful smile. His love had transformed her from a cowardly wife to a dutiful mother. Such a powerful love, it seemed capable of miracles.

Lise looked at her children. They were smiling, for the first time in days. They would believe anything if it came from his mouth, Lise thought. They all would. Murray's voice could heal all wounds. Yet as Lise sat there and listened to his slow, reasonable phrases, she suddenly realized that she had never been away from him for so long. Oh, he had gone to an occasional meeting, even to a conference or two, but never for more than a week. This was to be almost a month.

She would have to deal with his absence somehow. She was sure that she could figure it out. Henry would help her, and so would Gil and Diny. As long as she didn't have to leave them, she would be fine. And she wouldn't think about Murray leaving now, there was plenty of time for that; no, she wouldn't think about anything unpleasant when she could finally breathe because this ridiculous charade she had been living for the last several months was finally over.

The night Murray left was crisp and cold. Winter had been more severe than the predictions. April felt like February. Lise wore her new red winter coat and the children were in their heavy jackets. As Murray and she went over some last-minute details his overcoat billowed behind him and he appeared to be tilting toward her. Gil was too busy watching the planes, but Lise could feel Diny observing them, watching the way Lise kept plucking at Murray's coat. Lise didn't know why she was doing that, it was almost a nervous twitch, as if she couldn't bear to touch him and had to touch his coat instead. But she couldn't exactly explain it to Diny, or anyone. So it was a relief when the time was up.

The actual goodbye was confused. Murray had gotten permission for Gil to go into the cockpit and meet the pilot, and at the end they had to hurry. "Probably just as well," Lise said softly while they stood in the observation lounge waiting for Murray's plane to arc into the sky. "Goodbyes are hard. Better to say *au revoir*," Lise told her children. Her father had always said *auf Wiedersehen*. Yet Lise could not make her lips form the words.

They stood there, the three of them, with Lise's arms around her children's waists. Both Diny and Gil were taller than she was. My protectors, she thought, as they watched the curve of the plane's lights soar into the distance. Rays of light piercing the darkness, isn't that what travel is? Lise asked herself. Yet unlike that train that had sped past her home so many years ago in the deepest black of night, Murray's plane could have been Venus: a speck of light in the deep lilac of an April twilight. A faint pinprick in a sky still awash with blue.

At that moment Lise began to count the minutes until his return.

Diny, 1980

I remember my parents at the airport, their bodies forming two sides of a lopsided triangle as my father's tall body tilted toward her short one. I remember her touching the tweed of his overcoat as if it could yield some secret. I remember her holding our waists and her face looking intently into the sky as the plane went on its way.

Then we went back to our lives. Except for the calls from my father, things were quite normal—peaceful—as the weather changed rapidly from winter to summer, with hardly any spring at all. My mother had taken to sleeping later in the mornings that year and she was often asleep when Gil and I left for school; but during the time my father was away, she was up with us every morning, she was sitting in the living room reading when we came home, she was early and in the front row for the senior play, and she stood next to me on the exciting day when the letters from the colleges came. I can still see her gray eyes light up when I announced I had gotten into Swarthmore, my first choice, and I remember the fleeting veil of disappointment when she understood that I wasn't going to choose Vassar. The only thing that was different from our usual routine was her playing the piano for long hours in the evening. But she didn't have my father to talk to, and Gil was studying, and I was talking on the telephone, so she must have felt a little lonely.

I knew my suspicions were correct when I walked into the kitchen at the end of April and I heard my mother talking; she was making an appointment with Dr. Farnsworth. "I seem to need to know I'm going to see you a little more often while Murray is away," she was saying. My first instinct was to back out of the room. Although I knew she had seen Dr. Farnsworth for years, I didn't feel right, coming on her like this. But she motioned me to stay. After she hung up, though, she looked a little embarrassed. She didn't say anything then, and I told her about my day at school.

Later on, when I came downstairs to say goodnight she admitted, "I find I'm missing Daddy more than I thought I would." Her voice was sheepish. She had taken a bath and was in her nightgown and robe. The familiar fragrance of her bath powder floated up into my nostrils. On her lap was *The New English Bible.* After we had kissed, she put her leather marker into it and closed it. I loved to watch my mother handle a book or a piece of music; she didn't so much handle them as caress them.

Now she said, "I was reading Ruth. It's so short, I always forget how short it is until I read it again, but it's so beautiful, probably the most beautiful book of all." Then I noticed the dark rings under her eyes and I realized that the sounds I had been hearing for the last few nights, sounds I had ignored or thought were noises outside, had been my mother, wandering around the house, unable to sleep.

"Would you like some hot milk and honey?" I asked her. I didn't know what else to do, and that was her remedy and my grandmother's remedy for sleeplessness. But she shook her head and beckoned me toward her for another kiss, then said, "I'll be fine, Diny, don't you worry about me, I'll be fine."

But she wasn't fine, and a few days after that, she was waiting for us when we came down for breakfast. Her face was haggard and the ashtray was full of butts. I stared at her. I had never seen my mother smoke.

"I used to smoke a long time ago. Sometimes it feels good." Her voice was defiant. Then it sounded more normal, softer, "I heard mice in the cellar and they're still down there, hundreds of them." She shuddered and her eyes avoided mine. "Go look and see for yourselves," she told us. By now Gil had stopped getting his Cheerios and was staring at her with a queer look in his eyes.

In the cellar we could see only the constant ripple of some rolls of graphs wrapped in gray corrugated cardboard that my father had brought home from the lab a few months ago. One of the cellar windows had come open because the lock was old and rusty, and now the warm wind made a funny humming sound. Still, I could see why she had been fooled; if you didn't know what they were, the moving cardboard did look like the backs of mice or rats.

But she knew about those graphs, she had helped my father put them away, and she also knew about the cellar window.

We came up the stairs and as I bent to kiss her, to reassure her, I found myself repelled by the acrid, unfamiliar smell of smoke on her breath. "It's only some cardboard, there are no mice there, they wouldn't dare invade your clean house," I teased her. But all she managed was a short, odd laugh.

"There was also the woodpecker." Her voice accused us. Again we stared. We had heard about the woodpecker a few days ago as we had been hearing about it for the past two or three springs, but no one took that woodpecker very seriously. It had parked itself on top of a dying oak near the corner and no one, except my mother, got very excited about it.

Suddenly, I wanted my father. I wanted him sitting at this table, reasoning with her, explaining that the woodpecker needed to live, too. I hated to see her so dejected-looking, and now I wished she would go back to sleep. She obviously needed to get more sleep. Why were the mornings so hard for her? I wondered, then found myself wishing she were more like my friend Joan's mother, who was dressed in a skirt and fresh cotton blouse every single morning.

"Didn't you hear it?" she said.

"Sure, but it's not doing any harm, and besides, there's nothing we can do about it," Gil replied, pouring some milk on his cereal.

"No juice?" she asked.

"Later," he said, then looked as if he wanted to ask her why she was so interested in his breakfast. But he didn't.

"What do you have planned today?" she began, but before we could answer, she added, "Sometimes I wish you kids didn't have to go to school."

Just like that, out of the blue. I will never forget it. Nor will I forget my cold answer, "I have a senior assembly and Gil has a bio test—you remember that, Mom, you quizzed him for it last night." Talking to her as if she were a child.

I hated it, and as I stood there I wished I had a boy-friend, something, anything to make me forget my mother's face at that moment. Such an unhappy face as she stared at me with those penetrating gray eyes. So unlike her usual face. I hated to see that paleness, that grayness in her skin.

But before I could think of something to say, she straightened her shoulders and got up and pulled the sash to her robe tighter. Then she stamped out the cigarette and emptied the ashtray. "Of course, how stupid of me. I was only kidding, you knew I was kidding, didn't you?" Her laugh was still odd, but her face looked more normal, had more color in it. "Now go along, or you'll be late. And don't forget your juice," she said firmly to Gil.

By the time we left, she was standing at the door waving gaily. I wanted to run back and give her a kiss, my secret apology for those thoughts I had had about her only minutes ago. But there wasn't time.

At the bottom of the driveway Gil gasped. I turned. The magnolia had bloomed in the night, and now its blossoms burst with the most gorgeous pink I had ever seen. If only I could take my mother's hand and drag her down the path to see it. Once she saw that magnolia her spirits would lift. I could see her eyes glowing at the sight of the bush. But there wasn't enough time. The school bus was already grinding to a stop at the corner.

At the River, 1969

1

"Will that be all, Missus?" Andrew MacKenzie, who has owned the fish store for as long as she can remember, dangles the fish again. No rainbows glinting from the scales now, only gray sleekness. And Missus. When she was a girl he called her Liselotte, imitating her mother; when she married and they came to live here he called her LiseBranson, slurring it into one word; now that she is older, with this odd shock of white hair on one side of her head, he says, "How are you, Missus?"

"Beautiful day." Gina smiles and hands her change. She has known Gina since she was a child. Gina helped her mother with parties, like her graduation party.

"Say hello to the sun for me," Andrew says.

Outside it's hotter. Crazy, unseasonable weather, whoever heard of a magnolia sprouting blossoms at the very beginning of May? And overnight? Eerie. The blossoms didn't even look real, too perfect, plastic looking.

So hot . . . Usually she loves that radiant river light bathing the streets, but today it's too much, bleaching the

sidewalks and buildings to a paleness she's never seen before, and the air is actually throbbing around her. Yet she's
shivering. How can it be so hot and she be shivering?
Probably a hangover from this morning, when she woke
up chilled to the bone because of the woodpecker. How
could one bird make such a ripping, gunlike, hideous
sound—the sound of this decade, she suddenly realizes—
that incessant hammering into the tree as inexorable as
gunfire. Thinking of it she feels a cold sweat covering her,
like a thin layer of transparent jelly, dampening her blouse
and the lining of her coat, but it doesn't matter. Old coat,
much too long and heavy, she should have given it away
years ago. Why on earth is she wearing this ancient coat
today, dressed for March, not May, but still, how could
it be so hot this early in May after that cruel winter, scary,
this unseasonable heat . . .

If only she had listened to the radio. If Murray were
home she would have known not to wear it, but she doesn't
have the strength to listen to the radio so early—all it is
is trouble: someone killing someone else, people setting
bombs or fires, one country raiding another, and always,
like a song you can't get out of your head: Vietnam.

Once Murray told her that in China they announce
good things on the radio: This morning half a million
people safely crossed the main street in Peking. Things
like that, which make more sense, a much better way to
begin the day . . .

All winter you wait for some heat from that fickle,
watery winter sun, but then when it comes, it's a huge
hand pressing at the back of your neck. There, that's better—no one will mind her leaning against this pole.
Eleven-twenty, her watch says, an Omega Seamaster, Murray's old watch that slips all over her wrist because it's too

big, but she put it on this morning because she likes the weight of it, the knowing it is there, as if his hand were on her wrist . . . Eleven-thirty now. Surely she can spare half an hour to sit under the beech tree; all she has to do is get some fruit and salad and be at Henry's at three—hours and hours till then. Maybe she'll treat herself to lunch in the new natural foods store. Besides, why live near the river if you never take time to explore it? Papa had the right idea, he took a walk here almost every night, winter and summer.

And only last week, Henry said, "You should allow yourself more small pleasures." She wanted to tell him about a painting she saw years ago called *Small Pleasures,* but there wasn't time, the hour was up. And next to it, a drawing called *Delicate Joy,* though she can't remember the artist or any of the other pictures, only those two with those lovely titles and herself and Murray standing at the top of the Guggenheim watching the light filter through that dizzying space . . .

Of course Henry's right, he's always right, and she does deserve more pleasures than she allows herself, but joy is so delicate, so much more fragile than she could have believed when she was young. She'll tell that to Henry, that's the sort of observation he likes.

But what about the fish?

"Forget something, Missus?" Andrew asks. Gina stares with her black olive eyes, but Andrew's are as steady as a beacon, never surprised, not even now, just wondering.

"No, no, but I want to go for a walk and I didn't want to carry this poor fish around. Can you put it back on ice? I should be back in an hour—yes, I will, won't I?" But Andrew merely nods, not even puzzled by the question she never intended to ask.

"Sure, Missus, a walk sounds like a fine idea, and an hour should do it," he says. "Wish I could take a walk today, the leaves are just out and that young green that lasts only a day or two."

Young green. How perfect. And now she can feel a wisp of a breeze, surely it will be cooler down near the river. If only she could stop hearing that woodpecker . . .

At the corner, Sergeant Mulcahy directs the children going home for lunch. They're overdressed, like her. One is saying, ". . . and this afternoon maybe Mommy will turn on the sprinkler," and Lise can see their bright eyes and small chins lifting eagerly into the spray. Compared to her children, these little faces still look so new . . .

He motions her across. She sniffs. Some days you can smell the salt, but all she catches today in this shimmering heat is car fumes. Mulcahy makes her nervous when he stares at her like that—through her, almost—though God knows she should be used to it. She's known him forever; she first saw him the day of her graduation party, when his wife gave birth to a stillborn.

Then the butcher, the greengrocer. Baskets of strawberries glisten in the sun: "Buy me," they say. On her way back. Should she stop and tell him? No, no need, she'll be back before he sells out. Then the upholsterer, the shoe store man, the candy store man—all putting their faces into the sun. "Hello, Missus Branson. April felt like January and now May feels like July," they say.

At the next corner the stores stop and houses sit proudly behind hectic flower gardens. People along this strip have lived here forever and are known for their green thumbs. One woman even Mama envied, for she had dahlias taller than Lise. And the roses! River air must be good for roses, but there are too many red ones here for her taste.

When Rose saw the roses in Honeywell she said, "They must spray," but she was wrong. Such exuberant roses don't come from spraying, Mama never sprayed a rose in her life.

Nothing left of her mother's roses, even the fence at the south end of the garden is gone . . . They didn't build the A & P after all, but these garden apartments . . . She can hardly bear to look—boxlike buildings and horrible little overcultivated plantings, rhododendrons whose leaves look like cigars when they curl up in the winter, and those dull evergreens that scream suburbia. No, she won't think of it, she can't . . .

Above, the trees drip with buds, an umbrella of green encloses her, and when she steps from it she sees the river: a swath of brownish blue—no whitecaps, but it's not still either. She hates to see the river as still as glass when the whole point of a river is to see it move.

Finally, she's at the beech, she's known this tree since she was a child. It's the biggest tree she's ever seen, but now it's supposed to be dying, they're starting a fund to save it and this raggedy old park around it, but that beech can't be dying. It looks the same as always, indestructible. "Don't believe everything you read in the papers," Murray always cautions, and now she sees thousands of buds. By tomorrow there will be an explosion of leaves. Was this tree here when Hudson came? Besides, the magnolia at the bottom of the driveway was supposed to be dying a year ago, and when she passed it this morning, its swollen blooms were a thick milky pink Rubens would have given his life for . . .

Quietly the water curls toward shore, not very noisy today, but you can see a definite tide. Slowly, surely, the water creeps back over the tidal marks it just made, such a soothing rhythm, she loves to watch it, she feels as if an eraser is being pulled across her mind. Now she can hardly hear that damn bird . . .

Maybe she should get out of the house every morning. Suzy says she loves going to work. How strange: Suzy, who didn't work when her children were small, is now working, and she, who couldn't dream of not working, is now at home. Maybe if she had to work it would be different, maybe she wouldn't mull so over everything but put her feet on the floor and get dressed and start the day. Maybe Abe Goodside is right when he says she should start now, before Diny goes away.

But then there's Henry. "You don't need the money, Lise, and we must remember that working is pressure," he tells her. "You're almost fifty, you know." Forty-seven isn't fifty. Sometimes she hates him.

But they're growing up so fast and are not at all dependent. So she didn't spoil them, after all. And maybe pressure is exactly what she needs. It wasn't only the woodpecker or the mice—how stupid of her not to realize that those pieces of cardboard weren't mice or rats, either—it was the way the kids looked at her this morning, that queer look that said, "Let's get out of here as fast as we can."

Do they know that some days she can hardly see their beautiful faces because her mind is so cluttered with ghosts? Please God, don't let them know!

If only she could get up more easily, be more cheerful, but she's so exhausted from those dreams racing through her brain—an avalanche of dreams. Still, Henry said she was doing very well, whatever that meant, so instead of thinking about a job, she'd better concentrate on making the mornings better . . . Tomorrow will be better . . . It has to be. And now she has this pleasant morning near the

river, that's a lot to be thankful for, being able to walk
out of the house to the river . . . That's what she wanted,
isn't it? There, that's cooler. Her arms are finally out of
those heavy sleeves and her old coat makes a nice backrest
against this rough old tree . . . Now she can feel the breeze,
so maybe she can doze a little and when she gets up her
thoughts will surely be straighter . . .

2

The relentless glare rolls her eyeballs to the back of her
head, and the sun is a glittering bowling ball. So she
shields her eyes and looks down because you can go blind
that way, at least that's what they told them when they
were children. Now the debris rises and dances before her
eyes: shards of colored glass, crumpled soda cans, paper
bags polka-dotted with grease, some pennies that catch
the light, an old sneaker. If only she were still lying under
the tree, so pleasant to stretch out and listen to yourself
breathe and watch the pale leaves blink in the sun. Not
pale. Young. Young green. Beautiful.

Now some birdsong—a cardinal's whistle, or an
oriole? She can't tell, she's not as good as Murray and Gil,
but she has no time to wonder because she has to find her
bag. She can't believe it, but when she went to reach for
a tissue, it was gone. No one took it—no one was around,
and no one but Vittorio ever came to this old park anyway,
and he didn't take it. From where she is standing, Lise
can see Vittorio's small house. She had gone to school with
Vittorio, and like everyone in Honeywell, knew his craggy,
homely face and wonderful, welcoming smile. He was
supposed to be writing a book about the Hudson; he con-

ducted experiments with the water and the fish; he had visited Lise several times in the last few years and had taken notes from her father's notebook called *The Hudson.* No one knew how he managed to keep himself alive, yet he never looked hungry and wore immaculate work clothes.

No, Vittorio wouldn't take her pocketbook. But where is it? She had it when she passed Mulcahy, she switched it when he looked at her, but she didn't seem to have it when she went through the squeaky iron gate to the park, so she must have dropped it before that.

She'll start at the river's edge and climb the hill and look around the shortcut in the dump. The kids said there was poison ivy there, but she didn't see any; besides, she must be immune, she's never gotten it. Just as well the sun is so bright, that will make her keep her eyes down, all she needs is to rake the ground with her eyes and she'll find it. If she doesn't panic, it will be there right in front of her and then she can stop and take her shoes off and shake them free of the gravel that's gnawing at her stockings and soles.

It's not the money. She has only about fifteen dollars; she never carries a lot of cash since Sylvia Farnsworth was mugged in Tarrytown. It's the pictures, the children's and that old snapshot of Murray that she took one morning five years ago—maybe ten, time goes so quickly—and he was wearing his old windbreaker and he had forgotten to straighten the collar of his shirt before he zipped his windbreaker, so there it is: a piece of collar stuck into the zipper and every time she sees the photo she wants to reach out and fix it . . .

Now she can feel herself getting numb, too much standing, as if parts of her body are disappearing. She's not as young as she used to be, used to be able to walk

for miles in the sun, but no more . . . There, it feels good
to have the knob of her wrist in the small of her back;
there, if she rubs it she'll feel better; and yet when she
closes her eyes she can feel the sun's sting, and her eyes
throb and then something beyond the throbbing, a floating
almost—such lightness!—remarkable really. But then it
passes and she has her feet planted on this gravelly ground
and she opens her eyes, but if she had her sunglasses the
light couldn't play such tricks.

Of course. They're in her bag.

All she has to do is keep her head. Then she'll find
it. Her vision is excellent, and she never loses things.
"Your eyes are improving with age, Mrs. Branson," the
eye doctor said. "How lucky you are," the girl in the beauty
parlor said, "you still look good, I guess because you're
thin."

Oh, why is it so hot? A swollen tongue is growing
inside her head, she can barely swallow; and her coat drags
her down, she could be wading through sand. If only she
could go back to the tree and rest. But how can she stop?
She must find her bag, such good leather, practically new,
and that photo inside it. Other photos of him are simply
flat pieces of paper, only this one makes him real, gives
him a shape and body, a face and a smile . . . Oh, why
does she miss him so much? "A few weeks is hardly an
eternity," Henry said dryly. And Murray agreed. But she
misses him more than she could have ever imagined. For
the last few nights, she has lain wide awake, trying to
reconstruct his features: Sometimes she began with his
hairline and forehead and then his eyebrows, eyes, nose.
Or else she started with his chin and worked upward. But
she was working with invisible paint; as she made a stroke
in her mind, it disappeared. How can a face you have loved

for so long elude you? She can't understand it, yet every night, it was the same. Finally she would have to get out of bed and find her wallet and look at that snapshot so she could fall asleep.

"I want that bag," she says, and the sound of her voice is comforting. Then she makes a visor with her hand and peers along the edge of the water. Small fish are swimming, but that's an optical illusion, water brings things closer, those fish are deeper than they appear. "The Hudson has almost no shallow parts," Papa used to say.

"I want that bag. And when I find it I'll go back to Andrew's and then I'll walk home and see the kids and have lunch while they eat something." Her words float around her, some of the syllables break loose and echo above her head, but at least she has a plan. It's always better to have a plan. Besides, she's getting hungry. Why didn't she buy a pear, or some of those luscious strawberries?

A whistle curves into the stillness—long, low, too loud for a bird, too sustained. It must be a train going to New York. She tried to keep track of them before, but now she's lost it. It must be almost two, though her watch said one-fifteen the last few times she looked—it never went more than a few hours, that's why Murray replaced it. But when she put it on this morning, she hoped maybe it would right itself, sometimes when you don't concentrate too much on things they do that . . .

Now a warm wind ruffles the water, fluting the waves, creating tiny iridescences here and there, small rainbows on the surface as the fish are churned up and skim along, Christmas tinsel in May . . . It's bluer now, almost violet in places, and the shifting of the sun has leached out some of the brown. But still it's so hot, sweat runs down her arms and between her breasts, and she'd like to take off her coat but she's afraid she'll lose it. She should have left it at the tree, maybe the bag is sitting there, but no, it couldn't be, she searched around that tree for almost an hour . . .

What she wouldn't give for a shower and some iced tea, she's more thirsty than hungry, and she wants Gil's stringy arms and Diny's softness around her, hugging her, but then she feels Arthur's eyes searing holes into her. Help me, Mommy! Help me!

It's no use. She's got to sit down. Stumbling to an old railroad tie, she hears the slow shuffling of her feet, so quiet now, and then she hears the woodpecker again: a hideous counterpoint to the rhythmic lapping of the river only a hundred feet or so from the tips of her new shoes. After she wipes her eyes, the back of her hand is smeared with eyeshadow. Stupid to wear eyeshadow in this heat, but she thought it would make her feel better; she'll scrub her face when she gets home.

Home! What an idiot she is. Of course! Go home. Diny has car keys and there's an extra set if she's not home, and cash in the top drawer of Murray's bureau. Surely six eyes are better than two. Besides, it's too lonely here, not a soul in sight, not even a tug furrowing the water, and the brow of the Palisades a resplendent purple . . . "O beautiful for spacious skies, for amber waves of grain, for purple mountain majesties, above the fruited plain!" That's what those cliffs are: purple mountain majesties . . .

When she squints, they come so close she can almost touch them, so different from the way they look at the end of winter with those monstrous ice-beards hanging from them. One killed a boy when she was about fourteen. "Spring thaw and he was mucking around and an icicle fell off and speared him, he never had a chance," people said. Now all she can see are green sprouts on the dark cliffs. Young green.

And the water is clearer, greener; it reminds her of that freezing lake in Minnesota the first summer after they were married. Such a lovely color, the water must be perfect, she thought and rushed in and was numbed from the waist down. How Murray laughed, but then he ran toward her and began to rub life back into her body, so how could she stay angry with him when all he ever needed to do was touch her and she was happy? But she surprised him and they went back into the water and swam, letting their bodies get used to the cold, moving in tandem for longer than he thought she could.

Another whistle tearing the silence. What is she doing, dreaming about the past when she has to go home and call Henry? She must have missed her appointment, and it's time to start making dinner.

What was it Murray said after they swam in that lake? "I feel as if I own the world." How stupid they were! How young! There's a judgment for that kind of idiotic happiness, no one in this world is allowed to be that happy.

And she doesn't look forward to Henry's icy voice when she calls. He hates broken appointments, he tells all his patients, but he's only human, all doctors are, they make mistakes, too. Papa always said that, he hated it when they tried to make him God . . . They didn't know Arthur was going to die. Only she did. The big head, that famous specialist, called her in and said, "I can't understand why you're so worried, Mrs. Branson, your son is in the best hands, and you need to go home and get some rest." A lot he knew. Never talked to her again, sent his lackeys in to tell her what was happening, averted his eyes when they passed in the halls. Then turned up at the funeral because he and Murray had gone to Harvard together—at least that's what Murray said—and when she went into a rage, Murray kept saying, "It's over, Lise, it's over, let it alone . . ."

She couldn't let it alone.

She still can't. Arthur was their brightest child, more sensitive than the other two, you can see it in his drawings, amazing drawings: conductors on trains, the city at night, a man playing the tuba in a parade. You can hear the oom-pah-pah when you look at it. If Arthur were alive he could draw Murray's face for her; she would have something better than this awful blur in her mind. The next time she goes to Henry she must bring him those drawings. He would like them, but she can't trust Henry, either. Who can you trust in this world? How could Henry have expected her to sleep with Murray after Gil was born? As if she could forget one child now that she had another? The continuing litany of lies—"Put it all behind you, it's past, Lise, forget it, it's over, try to live for the present."

Only Murray understood, that's why he put up with her for all those months, he knew how she felt but he didn't say a word, just waited until she was ready, until they were both ready. Because after Arthur said, "I feel so cold, Mommy," then closed his eyes and expired—that was the word they kept using—she felt as if someone had taken a grapefruit knife and scooped out her heart the way Andrew scoops out the slimy innards of his fish.

Oh, my God, the fish.

3

It took all Jim Mulcahy's strength to stand on this corner— duty the younger men didn't want—and watch who yelled at their kids, who had cigarettes dangling from their lips, who drove too fast and slowed down guiltily, who was well put together and who wasn't. But sometimes there were pleasant surprises. Like now, for here was Lise Branson. Such a little bit of a thing, but pretty as a picture even if she was pushing fifty. Still that graceful walk she had as a child and that didn't go with her skittish eyes. But her eyes hadn't been so skittish then, she had looked like she held the world in the palm of her hand. He used to hear her practicing the piano. "Damned good she was, too," he once told Dr. Branson.

Today she looked a little tired, scared almost. "Nice day," he said, louder than he had intended. She jumped a little and her eyes clawed his face and slid away. Then she nodded and changed her bag to the other shoulder. Probably hot, he thought, dressed in that big coat and stockings. Too hot for stockings, he thought, and then she was gone, down toward the river.

In the lull around two o'clock, Andrew asked Gina, "Lise get back for her fish?"

"No, but she'll be along soon. Her kids will be coming home from school, and besides, she must be sweltering in that heavy coat she was wearing. It's ninety-two."

Andrew nodded. Lise had never forgotten her fish; she had been coming every Thursday for years, and before that she used to come for her mother and draw pictures with her toe in the sawdust on the floor. She knew that fish wasn't going anywhere. It was perfectly safe, and on ice.

At three-thirty, Henry Farnsworth tried to call the Branson house. He let the phone ring thirty times, hoping that Lise was out in the garden, but then he gave up. How odd. Lise rarely missed an appointment, and never one she had specially made, but it was also unseasonably hot. A drastic change in the weather often made people forget, and maybe this was a sign that she was fine, better than she thought. By the time he had finished making the phone call Henry had convinced himself that Lise was meandering through a museum in Manhattan. Besides, who could he call? The police would think he was crazy to call so soon.

Lise can see the fish in its little brown bag waiting on ice in one of those cases at Andrew's. Waiting for her. And all this time she's been standing here looking into the past like some ancient nag wearing blinders.

"It's the present that counts," Henry says. Now she has to find the quickest possible way home. The hypotenuse. She looks around and sees a Pepsi-Cola truck parked near the station. Surely he won't mind giving her a ride, truck drivers are usually good-natured, if only he doesn't leave before she can get there. Here, it's easier to run along the edge of the water, but her feet are so slow, she's following them instead of telling them where to go. "You'll get there," Papa used to say when they hiked. "Just put one foot in front of the other and you'll get there."

If only that truck doesn't leave, let it stay there, please. Then there's that strange sound she's been hearing for the past hour or so, what is it? A tug? A catbird? A sad sound, like someone calling for help, it pulls her head around so she lets the truck out of her sight; and there, in the water right in front of her eyes, is a patch of brown, bobbing as calmly as you please. She can hardly believe it.

If only everything isn't soaked, if only the photo isn't ruined, it can't be ruined, please, oh please, make it dry. Surely her luck will hold out. "How lucky you are, with your eyes." And if the photos are wet she can dry them, string them across the kitchen—photos, her social security card, her blood donor card, Blue Cross card, all the paper

ones. And she doesn't care if Diny smirks when she sees
them. She probably doesn't know you can iron a photo.
Why, if people iron hair you can iron paper, she'll tell her
children, so they don't think she's crazy.

"Crazy mother," she says out loud. The words echo
a little. "Do you know you have a crazy mother?" she could
greet them one morning. She could have said it this morning when she was frightened that there were all those rats
in the cellar making that rustling noise—of course they
were right, of course it was those graphs rattling because
the cellar window had worked itself open. She shouldn't
have told them about the rats, or the woodpecker, either,
but why should she have to weigh everything she says?
Why can't she simply say to them: "There are days when
I feel crazy. You have a mother who was crazy once and
sometimes still is"—the truth?

But how can she? At this late date?

Sometimes she thinks the hardest thing about her life
is not that Arthur died or her madness, but this lie. Per-
petuating this lie, this tangle of lies, really, that has become
woven so tightly there is no way on earth to unravel it.
Your mother is fine, your mother is like everyone else—
that's what they think, and perhaps that's right. It's wrong
to make children worry about parents, that's the parents'
job: to worry about the children.

But now that they're older, there are days when she
would like to confess, blurt out the whole business, admit
that she needs to see Henry, tell them she's on a drug for
depression, confess to them that she was once in an institu-
tion. "This is not an insane asylum," one of the women
used to chant. "This is a loony bin, a nuthouse, a funny
farm." Sometimes Lise can hear that voice coming at her
in her dreams.

Should she say, "You have a mother who was crazy," making it sound as casual as the fact that she has red hair, or gray eyes, or likes to read? No, the worst thing that can happen to kids is that they worry about a parent. When she was in high school, she had a friend whose mother lay most of the day behind drawn shades. The house smelled, not of dust or airlessness that had to do with furniture or rugs or food or lack of ventilation—or maybe everything to do with them, but she didn't know that then. All she knew was that the house with that bitter smell meant a sick mother. And when the mother did emerge, she had papery skin covered by an inch of powder and dyed black hair that had been plastered down by the worried palms of her friend and the friend's older sister and their amazingly cheerful father. But the eyes were the worst: dark eyes as distant as stars. Now Lise remembers how her friend's eyebrows—black, unplucked, young—would fall into a shallow V of worry when her mother appeared and began to speak in that strange elliptical way she had, her voice always a little higher than it should be, her syllables like needles plunging into her child's eyes, creating pinpricks of pain that no one would ever forget.

No, she will not do that to Diny and Gil. That is a prison sentence for children. No, she'll do it her own way, even if it means lying. There is no choice. Even Papa would understand that she can't be truthful under these circumstances. And what is it Henry once said? "If you have no choice, you do what you must. If you are expected to lead a normal life, you can."

Still, what does he mean by a "normal" life? She has no idea.

Crazy, mad, insane, loony, nuts. Yes, they are the right words, that woman was right. But they don't describe her anymore—how wonderful that she can say it. She's well now, and if she takes a pill every morning, well, so do lots of other people. So maybe now is the time to tell them. No, she mustn't tell them, it's bad enough that the world is crazy. "We'll never see anything again like the 1960s," the commentators are saying. They're right. But she knew that when they began this decade by building that horrible Berlin wall. That was the beginning, then Vietnam and Kennedy, and all those kids flipping out and the drug murders and Malcolm X and King. Will it ever end? they thought, and then Bobby. Crazy frightening world. No wonder she sometimes thinks there are rats in the cellar or a woodpecker is trying to kill someone. She's entitled. "Almost fifty isn't young, you know . . ."

But now the woodpecker is gone. Maybe this will be her lucky day. She lifts her head and can hear all kinds of other sounds, new sounds, no, just one—a pale shimmering sound that weaves through the air. Birdsong? Whippoorwills? No, too early in the day for them. No, these sounds are like bells, but there aren't any bells in Honeywell, it's probably her imagination . . . No, here it is again—clear pinpricks of sound . . . luminous crystalline sounds pouring into the air . . . beautiful arcs of sound calling to her: Come home, come home . . .

The truck is still there and the river as calm as a bolt of gray silk stretched across the dining room table waiting for Mama to cut into it. A wonderful stillness fills the air. It must be later than she thought; this is how the river gets at dusk when the day expands, grows enormous, embracing everything in it before it dies. . . Yes, the light is lower now, the Palisades are browner, that rust color they get in summer toward evening, and a breeze as cool as water spills across her skin . . . Her coat isn't so heavy now, she's glad she didn't leave it back there at the tree, it doesn't bother her at all as she starts to run in order to catch that truck . . .

4

She came up like a cat behind him, so quiet he almost dropped the carton of empties he was carrying. She could have been an angel with the sun beginning to descend behind her and those bells ringing—like background music—but when she said, "Can you give me a ride up the hill?" he saw that she was older than she looked. They climbed into the truck, but just as he was turning on the ignition, she stared at him with terror in her eyes; he thought at first she was having a heart attack. And a low whimper escaped from her throat. Then she whispered, "I've got to go back, I've lost my bag, and I must find it, otherwise the statistics will work against me. They do that, you know, if you've had a heart attack you're more likely to have another, and if you have cancer, you'll probably get it again . . ." Then she stopped and said in a more normal tone of voice, "Do you have the time?"

The truck driver told her it was five, and she sat there resetting her watch as if she had all the time in the world. Then he saw how messy her hair was and how streaked her face had gotten. Awful dirty for a grown woman, he thought, as she put her hand on the door handle and said, "Thanks for the ride, but I'd better go and find my bag."

He shrugged. He hadn't given her a ride. After she ran some of the way toward the river, she put her arms out to keep her balance. Her small silhouette receding into the distance looked like a dancer swirling. And she sure can run fast, he thought, then swung the truck around and headed for Honeywell. At the police station he told the old sergeant about the woman.

It must have been Lise Branson, Mulcahy thought as he logged in his hours for the day. Awfully late for her to be down by the river, though. On his way home he took a detour and stopped at the old park near the station. It was empty. That kid must have gotten his times mixed up. But that tree that everyone was fussing about looked more alive than he was. By tomorrow it would have burst into bloom.

Her heart is pounding in her ears, but she can't leave the river until she knows the exact place where she last saw her bag, otherwise she'll look like a fool to the kids and that's the last thing she wants . . . She felt foolish enough bothering that truck driver, but she must go back and mark the spot and watch the current so she can tell Diny and Gil exactly which direction it's drifting when they come back to get it.

She hoped he'd wait for her but he said he was late already, and then she must have scared him when she changed her mind. Besides, you can't ask too many favors of strangers, not now anymore, so she'll have to walk home, which should take about an hour. But the bag won't move that much because the river is almost glass, and when it's like that it's a tortoise. Patches of cloud are moving lazily now . . . It's what the radio calls basically clear, which amuses Murray because it doesn't tell you anything . . . But it doesn't matter what the weather will be as long as the bag doesn't move very far . . .

Yes, there's the splotch of brown and it hasn't moved at all, so maybe what the local people say about the tide isn't true. "A lot stronger than it looks," the fishermen used to tell Papa, who said, "I wouldn't believe everything I hear. People sometimes like to make nature more dangerous so their own lives will seem more exciting."

If she draws an imaginary line from the brown patch and kneels down she can make a marker with these stones ... Her stockings are in shreds anyway, and she can feel her big toes poking through them from all that running. The stones are still warm from the sun and feel so good in her hands, a perfect marker, what Papa used to call a "cairn" when they went hiking. Now nothing breaks the smooth surface of the river and the waves curl slightly, a small movement of that lip of water as they reach the shore ... And at her feet the stones are as smooth and warm as the inside of a child's forearm, and her eyes can draw a line into the water, and thank God, the brown rectangle is still there ...

It's time to go and find her children and then they will come back and get her bag. But oh, how her shoes pinch when she stands up, she never intended to wear them the whole day, no one in her right mind wears a new pair of shoes all day, certainly not at her age, but she doesn't want to be bothered carrying them either, and once she starts moving they don't hurt so much ... Now she has to hurry because here are some new sounds, different from what she's been hearing, not as strong as the bell-like sounds but lovely, tantalizing sounds ... Maybe the fish are singing. If dolphins can talk why can't fish sing? ... that's not so farfetched especially since these are such radiant sounds, Pied Piper sounds, a little clearer now, and she has the feeling that if she waits and doesn't panic she'll be able to figure them out ...

She moves a little closer, and now the pinching is

gone so she can concentrate. And the sky is suddenly pinkish red . . . as red as Wahrhaftig's legs . . . and she realizes they're voices . . . How could she be so stupid as to think they belonged to fish when they're ordinary human voices? . . . Voices she knows . . . and they're talking to each other in German and she can understand them as she always has been able to and now she's getting all the phrases even though they're speaking so rapidly. Mama has finished the pieces for that gray silk suit, and they're going marketing and she's repeating the list: strawberries, peaches, lettuce, rice, salt, baking soda . . . Don't forget the strawberries, Arthur, dear, they're so beautiful at this time of year, and remember to take Liselotte with you . . . Are you coming, Liselotte, please don't dawdle, sweetheart, Papa's in a hurry, he has hours soon . . . Her voice flows so easily, as easily as gorgeous music, like the slow movement of the Waldstein or Schubert's posthumous in A major . . .

. . . but now they've lost something . . . she can't make out what it is but she can help them find it . . . that's the beauty of having someone with young eyes along . . . and she has always had the best eyes in the family . . . so lucky with her eyes, the eye doctor told Mama only last week, so she calls, "I'm coming," and they slow down a little and she listens some more and realizes they are counting out some money for the shopping and she can understand everything, even the numbers, and she's astonished that at last she's found them . . . and she must follow them because they're old now . . . she can tell by their voices, which are as highpitched as children's when they're excited, and she can carry their packages and they will be so happy to see her . . . too many years since they were all together and they were always happiest then . . . and now as they start down to the village Papa recites, *Sein Blick ist vom*

Vorübergehn der Stäbe so müd geworden, daß er nichts mehr hält.
Ihm ist, als ob es tausend Stäbe gäbe und hinter tausend Stäben
keine Welt . . .

. . . so you see, it's true what she keeps telling Murray
that she doesn't need Rose and Harry or even George, she
can manage on her own now that her family . . . oh, how
wonderful it is to hear him say those words again: *Der*
weiche Gang geschmeidig starker Schritte, der sich im al-
lerkleinsten Kreise dreht, ist wie ein Tanz von Kraft um eine
Mitte, in der betäubt ein großer Wille steht . . .

. . . imagine finding them after all these years and
right here where they've been all the time taking a walk
near the river . . . when she calls out to them the German
syllables slip off her tongue as if not a day has passed since
she used them . . . she calls a little louder now . . . now she
can't wait to see their faces when they realize it's her . . .
they have no idea and Papa is still reciting "The Panther":
Nur manchmal schiebt der Vorhang der Pupille sich lautlos auf—.
Dann geht ein Bild hinein, geht durch der Glieder angespannte
Stille—und hört im Herzen auf zu sein.

. . . and she is so delighted she can't worry if it delays
her . . . the children and murray will wait . . . even arthur
will wait . . . and surely henrywillforgive her when he
hears . . . of course he'll have to forgiveher when he hears
shehasnt lost her german . . . not awordofit . . . notasyllable
. . . afterall . . .

The Long Night, 1969

As Sergeant Mulcahy was leaving the park, he saw Vittorio approaching. In Vittorio's hands was a brown pocketbook. Mulcahy peered into it, surprised at its neatness: a wallet, a leather photo case, a credit-card holder, tissues, keys, an embroidered handkerchief, and a loose snapshot of Murray Branson. Of course! He had seen it bouncing on one hip, then the other.

"Where'd you find it?"

"Near the dump. There's that shortcut to the park through there."

Mulcahy nodded. Lise Branson had been looking for her bag. Well, now she would have it back. He would take it to her himself. And he would warn her about the poison ivy. The last thing she needed, at her age, was poison ivy.

While Mulcahy was driving to the Branson house, Gil was rummaging through the refrigerator. "She went to the city and decided to take in a movie," he told Diny. Then, "Why isn't there any food in this house?" He opened the fruit bin. Two tired pears and a cantaloupe. Diny suddenly realized that her mother had scarcely shopped this last week.

"Want some?" Gil held out a piece of fleshy orange fruit. Diny shook her head. "Believe me, Diny, she's in the city. I'll bet you five bucks she comes home and tells us how nice the garden at the Museum of Modern Art was."

"But she never does that without leaving a note and dinner. Her bed wasn't made, there were dishes all over the table when I got home, and the milk and Cheerios were out." Somehow, she couldn't tell him she had also found a browning apple core on the floor near their mother's chair. "I also called the library and no one had seen her."

For the first time in years, Diny wished they lived on Riverside Drive, near Suzy. But Suzy was away this week anyway; she had called to tell them she and Stanley were taking an unexpected vacation. As she sat there, Diny realized that everyone was away. Rose and Harry had gone to Europe, and their neighbor, Doris, was visiting her new grandchild in California. That left George. Suddenly Diny realized that they hadn't seen George and Joanna since their new baby was born. They had moved from Riverdale to Westchester, Diny knew, but when she went to look up their new number in her mother's address book, it wasn't there. That seemed strange, but she didn't say anything to Gil.

Now Diny knew she shouldn't have gone to school. Why had she? She didn't have to. That assembly had been a joke; besides she had known this morning that something was wrong, but she went anyway. Why? The truth, she told herself, was that she didn't want to listen to her mother go on and on about the woodpecker, that she felt frightened when she saw her mother smoking and gulping her coffee, that she hated it when her mother looked like an old Raggedy Ann doll, so saggy and droopy. But she was ashamed to admit any of that to Gil.

Now he was staring at her, and she wished she could think of something, anything to say, when the ring of the telephone cut into the silence. Gil grinned. "I told you so," his eyes said. He didn't think she had enough faith in their mother. But that wasn't true. Diny was just more critical of her than Gil was, for no other reason than she was a girl. She loved her as much as he did, and she worried about her more than he did, that was sure. If she sometimes yelled when she was angry at her, that didn't mean Diny didn't love her. And Diny was so proud of her. Who else's mother had read all of Agatha Christie and Shakespeare and remembered the plots of both? And what about all those other books she read for her courses? Those seventeenth-century poets and the Bible and those journals she was always poring over? No one else's mother knew so much about biology or people like Peter Medawar, who her parents said was one of the smartest men alive.

Still, Gil was right in one way: Diny was still mad at her mother for not going to Japan. She guessed she would always be angry at her for that.

He let the phone ring once more. But when he picked it up, his face fell. Diny could hear a man's gravelly voice, "Hello, is that little Gil?"

"Yes, Andrew," Gil replied, frowning.

"Tell your mama she forgot to pick up her fish. I'll save it for tomorrow."

"Hey, wait, Andrew. Mom's not home, when did you see her?"

"She bought some bass this morning, before noon, then she came back and said she was going for a walk. But she never returned."

"Did she say anything about going to New York?"

"No, she said it was so nice out she wanted to go for a walk."

"Okay, Andrew, thanks. She'll get it tomorrow," Gil mumbled, then shrugged, as the doorbell rang. Oh, the relief! They ran for the front hall, envisioning her grayish green eyes and hearing her laughter already cascading down their spines. "Wasn't it silly of me to forget my keys? Will I ever get organized?" she would be asking them.

But when they flung the door wide, there was red-faced Sergeant Mulcahy hulking over them. In his thick hands was their mother's new Coach bag.

The river was a deep violet. As deep as an ocean here: "a drowned river," the geologists called it. Vittorio sat down on an old railroad tie, then took out his flask and wet his whistle. He never drank at home, too lonely; but here, with the river for company, a few drops wouldn't hurt. Then, as he wiped the top of the flask and returned it to his back pocket, he had to twist his upper body slightly, and a crumpled heap of blue or black entered his vision. Yes, a dark blanket, or a coat. His face blanched as he approached it, and his nervous cough reverberated in the dusky silence.

Diny had never called Dr. Farnsworth, but his number was the first *F* in her mother's address book. First a maid, then a woman's voice, "Diane, this is Mrs. Farnsworth. The doctor isn't in now. Is everything all right?" Diny told her the story of breakfast, then how she had come home and found everything so messy. But again, she couldn't make herself mention the rusty apple core.

"Was there a note?"

"No, and I threw out the milk and butter, then Gil

came home and Andrew from the fish store called. He said she came in around noon and said she would be back, that she was taking a walk, but she never came back." I sound like an eight-year-old, Diny thought, giving her all these details.

"Maybe she forgot the fish and decided to have a day in the city. Dr. Farnsworth has often told me how much she likes the city."

"But she has no money. The police sergeant came a little while ago with her pocketbook. He said someone found it in the old park near the river." Silence.

Then a breezy voice. "Try not to worry, Diane. I'll have the doctor call as soon as he can. Have you eaten?"

"Yes, we're fine. There's plenty of food," Diny lied. Then she said, very slowly and clearly, *"But she has no money."* Why was this woman so thick?

"I know, I know. Try not to worry, dear. We'll call you as soon as we can." Then she was gone.

Diny felt guilty about watching one sit-com after another, but she and Gil couldn't stop. What else was there to do? They couldn't leave, in case she called or came home. And they couldn't concentrate on their homework. Every now and then Gil's horselaugh would resound off the paneling and wood floor, reminding Diny that she and her mother had talked about getting a rug for this room. Something to muffle Gil's laugh, the same laugh as their father's. Murray. Diny could see him as clear as day. What she wouldn't give to have him standing in the doorway. But of course it was empty.

At eight-twenty Sylvia Farnsworth told her husband Lise Branson was missing. He didn't really react until she said, "Someone found her handbag near the river. A policeman brought it to the kids. Her wallet and everything else was in it."

"Call the Honeywell police and see if they know anything more," Henry said. When Sylvia called, the chief told her that Mrs. Branson had last been seen around five o'clock by a soda delivery man, but he didn't seem very concerned. "Her daughter seemed to think she had gone to the city. The kid wasn't upset at all." By now Sylvia was getting confused and angry, and when Henry called the Branson children a few minutes later, she wondered how he could be so calm. "I don't think the pocketbook is anything to worry about, Diane," he said, "your mother often comes in here pulling bills and change from her pockets, complaining that she'll never be organized." Sylvia could see Lise Branson's face, her eyes remorseful yet mischievous, like a naughty child who has no intention of changing her ways. She was a charming woman, with that lilting voice and its faint trace of accent. One of Henry's favorite patients.

Henry was worried, but he didn't want to transmit too much of his worry to the children. That was the last thing Lise would want. How important it was to her that the children believe she was fine! He had rarely had a patient so obsessed with the need to be a model parent. But perhaps that was what kept her going as well as she did. Still—he would be irresponsible if he didn't notify someone in the family, as well as the police.

"Is your Uncle Harry home?" he now asked Diny.

"No, they're in Europe. And I can't find Uncle George's new number; he just moved to Appleby," Diny replied. Her voice had a slight tremble. Henry made a note to call information.

Then he asked, "Would you and Gil like to sleep here tonight?"

"No, no," Diny answered, her voice stronger now. "We'll be fine, and we want to be here when she comes home."

"All right, but please call if there's a problem, and please let me know when she gets home—even if it's the middle of the night."

Henry called the police again. His voice was very firm, for he was expectng the usual police nonchalance about missing persons. But of course he had forgotten that the older policemen had known Lise since she was a girl.

"We're on top of it, Dr. Farnsworth. We have two cars cruising the river towns, we've alerted the railroad, and one of our men has gone to search for her in Grand Central Station. I knew her father, Dr. Hurwitz, wonderful man . . ." Then there was a pause. Henry waited. He could sense that the man on the other end was taking a deep breath. "Someone found a coat near the old park by the river. We think it may be hers."

Henry could feel his heart drop. His hands were clammy as he instructed the policeman to call him if there were any further developments. Then he called Appleby information and got George's number. He would wait just a little while—in his mind's eye he could see Lise walking from the theater district to the station, the money she needed neatly folded in her pocket, and it was much too hot for a coat.

Around ten-thirty, her eyes aching from all that television, Diny stood at the upstairs hall window and looked at the river. With the naked eye it seemed calm, still. Yet when she picked up the binoculars hanging on the hook nearby, she could see that it was getting rough, with darting flashes of light, which meant that the silverbacks were jumping. A storm was on its way. But for now, the sky was clear, the moon a glowing yellow disk. And warm. You never got that golden moon unless it was warm.

She and Gil lasted until eleven-fifteen. She knew there were still two more trains from New York, but she couldn't stay awake; her shoulder blades fluttered from exhaustion. She checked the front door, then the back. The key was in its usual hiding place, in a little pocket her mother had sewn on the underside of the mat. Lise hated locked doors, and they had never locked their door, even at night, until a year or so ago.

Then she called the police again to report that her mother was still gone. A new voice assured her that there were two cars out looking for Mrs. Branson.

"If she went to the theater, she could be on the last train," Diny said. The voice agreed and told her to call if there was any change.

Was her mother walking very fast somewhere, her head down, her eyes distracted? No, she would have realized the time when darkness fell, and she would have come home. Or at least called. She knew they would worry. But maybe she had gone to the city and was on a train gliding through the darkness right at this moment. Diny could see her dozing a little, then opening her eyes when the conductor chanted "Honeywell." And tomorrow her mother would be telling them about some terrific new play she had seen. Didn't she always say, "No news is good news"?

"Come on, Gil, time for bed." Diny shook him. When he opened his eyes, they were wide with pleasure. He thought she was Mommy. Then his face fell, and he tried to hide his disappointment. But Diny understood. In his place she would have felt exactly as he did.

Henry Farnsworth shuffled the pages of Lise's folder. He had seen her a week before. She wore a new blue-and-white-checked silk dress. He complimented her on it, and she blushed, confessing, "It was an extravagance, but I couldn't leave the store without it." Then she had frowned. "The trouble with getting a new dress is that then you need new shoes, too." Then she had laughed, and they had talked about her going back to work and Swarthmore, where Diny was planning to go, and her Bible course, and Robert Schumann, and Murray's absence.

"I miss him," she admitted. "*Physically.* Not just in bed, that's not what I mean, but in a truly physical sense, as if part of my body were gone, or maimed. I don't feel completely here," she had said. "But we're halfway there. He'll be home in less than two weeks." That was all.

And now she was gone—where, no one knew. So, you never know. Paranoia, complications due to menopause, repression of her real feelings to keep up this endless pretense for her children, God knows what. She could be safe, or she could be dead. He could not discount the possibility of real tragedy. In all the Greek tragedies the cause of trouble was hubris: pride, or some other such "noble flaw" in character. But in this century life wasn't so clear-cut—if it ever was—and tragedy wasn't so directly related to a perceivable cause. Tragedy often visited those who deserved it least, who had suffered from an accumulation of outside events totally beyond their control. The more he lived, the more he realized that a person's character had little influence over his fate. And the less faith Henry had in psychiatry and his ability to help change anyone's life. Not that he would admit that to anyone, but it was what he had come to believe. Especially in the really puzzling cases like Lise's.

Henry sat back and watched the trees and bushes cast their spectral shadows on the curtains in his office. Then he dialed George Branson's number.

Before George could reach across the bed, Joanna picked up the telephone, and the screeching ring stopped. What kind of animal would be calling strangers at this hour? It was almost midnight. Joanna handed him the telephone. "It's a Dr. Henry Farnsworth. He lives in Scarborough. He's Lise's psychiatrist."

The telephone was clammy against George's neck. He hadn't seen Lise since Thanksgiving. She was upset when she saw how much their new baby, Emily, looked like Arthur, and although he had seen Murray for lunch several times this winter, he and Joanna hadn't seen Lise and Diny and Gil. Yet now Lise seemed to be in trouble. Or this doctor thought she was. "Just a moment, Dr. Farnsworth, could you tell me that part again?" he said.

Okay. Lise's pocketbook was found near the river; she hadn't been seen since late morning by anyone who knew her; a man delivering soda to the station had seen her late in the afternoon; and Gil and Diny were alone in the house. Farnsworth had spoken to the cops, and they were looking for her. One had even gone to New York to search for her in Grand Central Station.

Then Farnsworth did a turnabout: He was saying that there might be no emergency at all, that Lise sometimes went to Manhattan and didn't come home till very late. With all the man's hesitations and interpolations, George couldn't get the sequence straight. All he knew for sure was that Lise was gone, the kids were alone, and this shrink on the other end of the phone was scared. George had never known Farnsworth, really, but from what he could remember about him, the doctor wasn't a man who scared easily.

"What do you want me to do?" George asked.

"I don't think there's anything to do. I just wanted you to know. I wouldn't be acting responsibly if I didn't let you know."

"Do you think I should call the kids, or go over there?"

"No, I think that might only frighten them more. And maybe we'll be lucky, maybe Diny's right and Lise will be home on the last train." Now Farnsworth's voice didn't sound so scared.

"Fine," George replied, "I'll speak to you in the morning."

A warm wind blew through the upstairs making the floorboards creak—soft fir floors that had been refinished for the last possible time, Daddy told them when they moved here, and for years Gil and Diny had wondered what nailheads had to do with it, why you couldn't get down to the nailheads, but they had never asked.

Gil woke from an old dream: He was on a beach and waves of sand were sweeping into his eyes and he was rubbing the grittiness from his eyes, and he had started to cry, but then Murray appeared, his large torso blocking the sun and his face bending toward Gil's as he wiped the sand from Gil's nose and eyes and lips. It was a dream as familiar to Gil as his name, and whenever he mentioned having it, Murray would say, amazed, "You were less than two when that happened, I can't believe you remember it." But Murray wasn't here this morning to say it, Gil thought, then slept again.

When he opened his eyes next, a thin stream of moonlight was runneling its way through a crack in the curtains and along the edge of his bed and next to the dresser and out the door. He could hear the woodpecker. Dawn must be near, because woodpeckers slept at night, or if they didn't sleep they stayed in their nests, so she heard it only after daybreak, which is far from a whole night. He hated it when she made such a fuss about that lousy woodpecker, as if it was the most important thing in her life. He didn't even mind it; its drilling had a rhythmic, low sound, like a heartbeat. A long *q* and then a *whirr—quwhirr,* it sang. *Quuwhiirr.*

Then not to remember his biology test after she had quizzed him for an hour the night before. He couldn't understand it. Then Gil remembered a conversation he had with his father before Murray left. "Try to be sensible and remember to do all the things you feel you must do. Mommy is stronger than she sometimes seems. People do what they have to do. Asking someone to stretch herself is better than letting her give in to herself."

So they had gone to school, even though her face had that odd blankness and those dark rings under her eyes that Diny thought had something to do with her period. And when they got home she was gone. And now she was still gone. For if she had come home she would have covered him with an extra blanket or lowered his window. So Gil lay there, shivering, unable to move—as if getting out of bed would be admitting something.

The Next Day, 1969

Muddy daylight filtered into her room. Diny opened her eyes, closed them, let the light ooze away, and slept once more in the sweet dark. The webbed light cleared as she widened her eyes. Hugging her bare arms, she stumbled into the hall. If only her mother were sleeping peacefully, the knuckles of her left hand pressed against the cleft of her chin, her reddish hair mussed around her heart-shaped face. Diny tiptoed expectantly over the threshold. Then her head clogged with confusion as she took in the empty, tightly made queen-size bed. She had made it herself yesterday afternoon, smoothing the sheets over and over, getting every crease out, as her mother had taught them to do so long ago.

Gil shuffled from his room. "What time is it?" he asked.

"Seven." Diny shivered. Gil put his arm around her and his blanket trailed behind them. Some King and Queen, Diny thought.

"Should we go to school?" he asked. His eyes were that flat black they got when he was scared.

"No." Diny couldn't imagine opening her locker, greeting her friends while her mother was God knows where. "No, we should be here when she gets home. Or calls. You sleep?"

"Yes," Gil said, but she knew he was lying. They looked away from each other and stood there, entirely separate, until the telephone rang. Diny rushed for it. "Oh, hi, Dr. Farnsworth," she said in a sinking voice. "No." Her voice was formal, almost cold. "We're very comfortable, thank you. No, we're going to stay here and wait, she should be along any minute, and I want to make fresh coffee." She hung up the phone. Then she turned to Gil. "Come on, Gil, what's the matter with you? We don't want Mom to walk into a mess." From his expression she knew she sounded like a bossy older sister, but she didn't know what else to do.

While Gil was in the shower, Diny went to the top drawer of her mother's night table. There was the key, which she then put into the keyhole of the top drawer of her father's bureau. She sighed with relief. Everything was as usual: the cash they always kept, an extra set of car keys, a few pieces of gold jewelry, She counted the money: four fifties and five twenties, as always.

Then she went to their bathroom and showered and used her mother's bath towel, though Mommy didn't like them to do that. It smelled of her perfume. What was she wearing? Diny wondered. They had last seen her in the blue nightgown and robe that hung on the hook of the bathroom door. Then it came to her. Maybe her mother had amnesia. Maybe she was sitting in some velvet maroon cave of a theater, or wandering around a neighborhood not far from here, unable to remember who she was. Diny had once seen a movie about a woman with amnesia who kept

riding around New York on the subway. But that happened
only in movies, she suspected, then let her fingers graze
the light batiste of her mother's nightgown.

They made an elaborate breakfast—eggs and bacon
and toast—and then gobbled it, and just as Gil was trying
to swallow the last bite, the ring seared the air. This time
it had to be her. Gil ran for the extension upstairs; he
wanted to be sure he knew where she was because Diny
wasn't very good at getting directions. How he wished he
could drive; if he could drive he had the feeling they
wouldn't be in this mess.

It was a man's voice, the same voice as Murray's.
Murray, their father, who was away. Or was he? Maybe he
wasn't away and she hadn't disappeared. Maybe this whole
horrible thing was a nightmare, Gil thought. But no. The
telephone was real and so was the made-up bed. Now the
voice said, "It's George, Uncle George." Wearily, Gil put
the telephone back into its cradle.

"They're coming over with their baby," Diny told
him when he came down the stairs. "George and Joanna
moved to Appleby. They have a new baby, a girl, you
remember, her name is Emily, we saw her at Aunt Rose's
on Thanksgiving," she told him quietly, as if he were
slightly retarded. Why am I acting this way? she wondered,
then asked herself once more why they hadn't seen that
new baby. After all, they lived only twenty minutes away.
Suddenly Diny was angry at her mother for ignoring
George's family, angry at her for going for her walk, for
behaving in this absurd way. What kind of stupid game
was this?

"Farnsworth called them last night and told them
about Mom and they're coming over to see us," Diny added.

As soon as he saw the little pile of stones in the course of his usual morning walk, Vittorio felt as if some elf or gnome from the Washington Irving legends were working its spell on him. So he wasn't at all surprised when, a few minutes later, he spied the shoes. Blue, too, and almost a quarter of a mile from where he had found the coat. A pretty blue, dew-stained, but with a little polish, as good as new. But so tiny. Five and a half. Maybe they had nothing to do with the coat. No grown woman had such small feet—why, his mother who was vain about her feet wore a six and a half. Maybe some little girl had gotten hot and left them there.

Then Vittorio told himself: Stop dreaming. You couldn't walk here barefoot even if you were a foolish kid, your feet would be cut to shreds. Besides, no kid in this day and age wore shoes like this. Quickly he pulled on his slicker. A sickle wind cut through the gray sky. Rain was right behind those clouds. And the temperature had dropped thirty degrees in the night. Within a few minutes he had reached the Honeywell police station.

The pink cuplike blossoms of the magnolia floated on the dewy gray mist. Diny watched them while she waited for George and Joanna; when they saw the marvelous bush, the worry in their faces disappeared, making their features look retouched. But then the concern returned, and the three of them walked solemnly to the house. Not even their baby, a dark-eyed, dark-haired baby who reminded Diny of someone she knew but couldn't place, could distract her from the reality of what was happening, why they were so abruptly here, and why Gil looked so angry when he opened the front door. "We don't need you," his eyes said to George.

But, of course, they did.

Joanna's gaze took in the living room, its flowered needlepoint rug, the comfortable sofas and chairs, and the shelves of books, the tulips and magazines on the tables, the old walnut Steinway. On the bridge of the piano was the piece Lise had played the night before last: "Gluckes Genug," and then underneath, in English, "Perfectly Contented." It was her mother's favorite of the Schumann *Scenes From Childhood,* and she had played it after she closed the Bible that was still on an end table with her bookmark in it.

"It reminds me of my parents' house," Joanna confided. Diny nodded and looked away. For now she could see her parents—Lise sitting and Murray lying down with his head on her lap and the strange circle of light around their heads. It should have given her comfort; instead it frightened her. The pretty room, the books and music waiting for her, the magnolia bursting outside—they meant nothing. For suddenly Diny knew what she hadn't known an hour before: Her mother had vanished and would not be found.

She looked at Gil, but he didn't yet understand. His eyes kept straying to the door. Her body heavy with the weight of what she now knew, Diny dragged herself through the room and turned on a few lamps. Suddenly it was dark; huge black and blue clouds were about to pull down the whole damn sky.

Now George was asking Gil how school was, what position he played in baseball, what sports he liked, his summer plans. Time fillers. Words skirting the surface of what none of them could express.

Suddenly George turned to her. "Who's your lawyer?"

She stared. "Jake Huber, Suzy's brother. Suzy's Mommy's best . . ." she started to say.

"I know Suzy. And Jake, too," George said, reminding

her that he had known their parents longer than Gil and she had. Diny began to breathe more easily. George was here, George would help them.

Then it was Diny's turn to talk about Swarthmore and the summer. As she answered their questions, Gil sat, his head bent forward, his elbows on his knees. His knobby wrists were inches from the edge of his sleeves. Had he grown two inches in the night, or was his shirt simply too small? Diny wondered, then noticed that Joanna was looking at her watch. The baby, Emily, had begun to whimper and was rubbing her eyes.

"She's late for her nap," Joanna was saying, and she frowned. "We really ought to get her home, George." George stared. "Maybe we can have the phone calls switched to our house; that way we can all go home," Joanna suggested gently.

Gil's head whipped around. "But someone's got to be here when Mommy comes home," he insisted. His words settled like dust on the surfaces in the room. But they were empty, meaningless words, Diny thought. *Pro forma* words that had nothing to do with the reality of what their lives had so abruptly become.

Diny liked George's house, its coziness, the eaved rooms, the hushed feeling of the carpeted floors, the built-in furniture, the small scale. She felt so much better that she thought perhaps she could eat. But once they sat down, she couldn't. Neither could George and Joanna. Gil was wolfing it down, though, as usual. She looked at George, then Joanna. Did they think Lise was some hippie mother who had awakened one day and decided to find her own space—something kooky like that? Diny wondered. Oh, where was she? Outside the sky was black and sheets of rain slapped the house. If she got drenched she could get sick, she was hardly ever sick, but sometimes she looked as if a wind could blow her away. And why didn't she come home? Diny couldn't understand it; her mother's favorite place on a rainy day was the living room sofa with a good book.

Now George was standing up.

"What's the matter?" Joanna asked.

"Nothing."

"Where are you going?"

"Back to the village. I need something." Diny knew he was lying, and as he and Joanna walked to the door she strained to hear "house," "nap," "lunch." But no "police." Not yet, anyway.

It unnerved George to see Gil so hungry, and while he watched the boy eat, he had realized they hadn't been as thorough as possible. They had put a note for Lise on the kitchen table. What if she came home so tired she went straight upstairs? She might even have assumed the children were in school, or she might be confused and think it was still yesterday. Anything seemed possible to George as he drove back to Honeywell.

Now the magnolia was bowed down by the wind, but its blossoms were still intact. That seemed nothing short of a miracle with the rolling thunder and jagged light. Maybe it was a good sign. But as soon as he opened the door, George knew no one was there. You could smell the emptiness. The note was where they had left it, and upstairs the bed was taut, untouched.

Folding Emily's diapers, for Joanna was doing everything she could to keep them busy, Diny tried to piece together what fragments her mind could hold. The truth.

She and her mother had had two fights in the last three days. The first was about a slumber party, and Diny had finally shouted, "But I'm almost eighteen and next year I won't even be here!" She had wanted to say a lot more, but when she saw Lise's pale face, her singed eyes, she had stopped.

The next day, her friend Joan had insisted that Samson was a book in the Old Testament, and Lise had corrected her, "Samson is part of the Book of Judges." When it turned out that Joan was wrong, Joan said, loudly, "Most people have better things to do than read the Bible or play the piano all day." And Diny hadn't said a word in her mother's defense, and later Lise's eyes stared mournfully at her. But everyone knew Joan was fresh.

Besides, Lise wasn't the only mother who didn't have a job. Actually she could go to work for Dr. Goodside anytime she felt like it. Diny knew that he called her every few months asking when she'd like to come back. And all the teachers always told Diny how smart Lise was, how well read. And she took care of the house and the shopping and laundry and all the cooking and the garden, and the finances, too.

Then Diny realized she had been saying all this aloud. Horrified, she bowed her head in shame. But instead of seeing her mother's triumphant smile when she returned, daring them to forgive her this unpardonable prank, Diny found herself wondering what time it was in Japan.

The boat pitched mercilessly. Now Vittorio wondered why he had said yes to the chief. He had never seen such an angry river at this time of year, and the two rookies with him were no help at all. The waves surrounding them were high as ocean waves. Vittorio knew that this spot was once shallow, but in the 1800s, it had been dug to almost thirty feet to make it navigable. And now they were in the midst of it. He needed all his strength to plunge the tip of the rudder into the waves and race the engine. But he knew they wouldn't find anything. The lightning and thunder had turned this river inside out: Odd bits of rubbish had been churned up from the bottom, and it was now a ferocious snake. As he steered the boat back south and to shore, he began to roll facts about the Hudson around in his head: 315 miles long, 75 million years old, on a bedrock of mica schist. It seemed the only thing his mind could hold.

While he was in Honeywell, George decided to go back to the police station. He and Joanna had stopped there this morning, but there had been no news of Lise. This time, the chief beckoned him into his office. The man's face was as gray as the wall behind him. "They just pulled a body out of the river at the North Yonkers station. Commuter saw it and called in. Must have awfully good eyes to see it in this muck. They didn't have to use grappling hooks; were able to get it from the side with a net. Didn't take long at all." He hesitated, and when he spoke again, his voice was almost inaudible. "It's a woman."

Tall, short, fat, skinny, what color hair, what kind of clothes? A hundred questions converged into a lump lodged at the back of George's throat. Slowly, he jotted directions to the morgue.

Then Sergeant Mulcahy burst into the chief's office. "I'll drive you," he announced. The chief looked startled, then nodded in assent.

The Morgue—for that was what the sign said on the door—was a long white room filled with white boxes that reminded George of the old-fashioned ice-boxes he knew as a child laid on their sides. White, thick-walled, but with intricate locks. The medical examiner, a plump, older woman, guided him slowly toward a stretcherlike affair. Then she gave an apologetic shrug and turned back the sheet.

George's first impulse was to say he had never seen her before. It would have been true. For Lise's fine, high cheekbones were obliterated by bloated flesh; her quiet intelligent eyes stared blindly upward; her bud of a mouth was now a bruise across the lower portion of her face; and her flattering, simple hairdo was matted and frizzed beyond recognition. Her blue-and-white-checked dress had been unbuttoned, then rebuttoned wrong, making her appear crooked, and the lower third of the dress was bunched around her pelvis, revealing white panties and a white petticoat wrinkled flat against even whiter limp thighs.

No one should be seeing her like this. It wasn't right, George thought, and then leaned forward in an attempt to set her to rights, to button her properly, but the strange woman gently touched his forearm and murmured, "Against the rules."

Then George scanned the rest of her: knees thickened slightly by use, the rolled, torn stockings that had worked halfway down her calves, the waterlogged ankles and tiny feet: swollen, bruised, her big toes poking through her stockings and pointing outward.

How could this be Lise?

He clamped his eyelids tight, and he could feel the grief rising in his throat.

Of course it was Lise. The long auburn lashes, even on the lower lids, the thin straight nose, that one slightly arched eyebrow making her forever surprised, that charming stubborn protuberance of her lower lip. Murray's old Omega on her wrist, and then those thin fingers—for oddly, the hands hadn't swelled—and on her left ring finger the gold band that matched Murray's. All splayed on a brown rubber sheet.

A terrible dryness overcame him. His head was wood. When the woman looked at him, George stared back, speechless. How could she do her job so calmly? She looked inquiringly at him. She waited. There were rules. Finally, George nodded.

That was all she needed. Thank God. She pushed a form toward him, handed him a pen, and made an X where he was to sign. Only after he had written his name did she cover Lise. Then a man appeared with a chair, George sat down, and the woman went to get Mulcahy. George watched the man who had brought the chair open one of the refrigerators; a body slid out as smoothly as a carton of eggs. Then Mulcahy was there, and they could leave.

George stopped in the driveway, pulled up the emergency brake, and opened the car door. He felt enormous—an oversize robot plunging through the air. The slam of the car door resounded through the drying air. Cirrus clouds swept the sky. The four-thirty whistle blew.

When he turned the knob of the front door, Diny and Gil were pulling it from the other side. George blinked. Diny watched a skin of saliva bubble across his lips, but she could hear no words. He coughed, and the bubble broke.

"It's her," he blurted. But they had no idea what he was talking about or where he had been. They stared. George wet his lips, but there were still no words. Yet he had to say something.

"Someone saw a body floating in the river. He was on a train going to the city. He called the police and I went to the morgue. It's her," he said.

"Oh, Diny, can you hear me, it's your mother, it's Lise," George pleaded.

Now Diny's mouth formed an O, but nothing came out. Gil stared at her and George leaned forward. Diny heard a streak of sound as harsh as tearing silk. Where was it coming from? she wondered, then she saw Gil's terrified eyes and she realized that that brutal sound had come from within her throat.

Suddenly she and Gil were moving. Together they lurched toward George. George was here, George would help them. The surge of their weight made George topple, but he caught his balance and leaned against the doorjamb. Before they knew it, Diny and Gil had fallen into his outstretched arms.

Diny, 1980

"It's her." That ungrammatical phrase echoed in my ears as I told George and Joanna I wanted to go home and call my father from there. I needed the familiar objects of our house around me while I did the hardest thing I ever had to do in my life. And although George offered more than once to make the telephone call, I shook my head. This was my responsibility.

As we turned into the driveway the magnolia was bent low, its branches bowed almost to the ground, encircled by the magnificent blossoms, more pendulous now from the weight of the water they held in their rosy petals. In the feathery mist the bush was more radiant than it would have been in spangled sunlight, yet how could so many petals be intact after that pounding wind and rain? But there they were, before my eyes.

And my mother was dead.

As soon as my father heard my voice, he knew that something terrible had happened. And when I said, stupidly, "Mommy's gone," he knew that *gone* meant *dead*. I heard the words *accident* and *drowned* leave my lips, but it was as if someone else were speaking them. Still, his voice helped me, just hearing his voice kept me calm.

When Murray came home, we talked endlessly about Lise's death. My father didn't have any answers, even when I pressed him. "We are visitors on this earth," he finally said once, when we were talking late into the night, "and she stayed as long as she possibly could."

At first his resignation angered me, and there were times when I thought he was excusing himself for what he had not been able to do. But then, I would ask myself: What if he had told us she was ill? What would have happened then? Might she have given up earlier? Might we have had a very different childhood? Might we have grown to hate her? I did not know.

By the spring of 1977, the three of us had gravitated to New England. Murray was teaching at Harvard, Gil was working in Maine, and I was doing graduate work at Brandeis. As I watched my father in Boston that spring, I had the sense that for him time had fallen away. In his mind he was once again the young man in the famous lab about to fall in love with that beautiful Dresden-like girl with the startling gray eyes who would become my mother.

We talked about it one evening while we were having dinner. He was astonished when I said it, and he nodded, "I look for her all the time," my father admitted, "and when I see someone very small with hair anything like her color, I find myself walking very fast. But when I catch up, of course, I'm disappointed." He said it so cheerfully that I envied him for the first time in my life.

A few weeks later, the two of us met for tea at the Ritz. It had been a favorite place of my mother's. With my father were two young men, his favorite graduate students, I realized, as I listened to them talk. One of them was Michael, whom I married two years later, in that very room. After I met Michael I was able to say, "My mother drowned and some people believe it was a suicide," for the first time.

But I can't say I believed it, nor could I ever get used to that phrase *commit suicide*. How strange words are. Once I read a line in a poem that said, "One must commit a painting the way one commits a crime." The poet was quoting Degas. I could understand that. You commit a sin, commit adultery, commit murder, commit suicide. Yet to commit yourself to something means to make a commitment—marry, take a job, have children, study so you can have a profession, be utterly convinced of the rightness of a cause.

Lise was committed to Murray, to Gil and me, to the work she hoped to go back to. So how could she commit suicide?

I didn't know then, and I still don't know.

Gil is married and works at Woods Hole, as a marine biologist. Murray is back in New York, still at Sloan-Kettering. He moved from Honeywell to an apartment on the east side. During the week he works very hard, and on the weekends he sees friends and reads and has begun to learn how to play the cello. Grandma Simone died two years after my mother's death, and we see my Uncle Leo and his family once or twice a year. On most of the big holidays, we all congregate at the Bransons' home on Long Island.

Now that the baby has arrived, Michael and I some-times drive from Manhattan to lower Westchester and take a walk along the aqueduct. Someone has begun to fix up the octagonal house my parents always pointed out to Gil and me when we were growing up, and our house is there, just as we left it.

The magnolia still blooms every year. So does the huge beech, and the hearts-ease.

Hundreds of miles north, the Hudson still flows from its tiny source.